GALENA'S GIFT

by Rosemary Nelson

Napoleon Publishing

Cover illustration and alpaca logo: Scott Chantler
Book design: Craig McConnell

Published by Napoleon Publishing
a Division of TransMedia Enterprises Inc.
Toronto, Ontario, Canada

Printed in Canada

05 04 03 02 01 00 99 98 97   5 4 3 2 1

Canadian Cataloguing in Publication Data

Nelson, Rosemary, date
        Galena's gift
ISBN 0-929141-56-3

I. Title.

PS8577.E39G34 1997   jC813'.54   C97-931442-9
PZ7.N44Ga 1997

For "Gamma Nar", the best
grandma and mother-in-law
in the universe!

CHAPTER 1

Alpacas! I don't want alpacas. I want a horse like you promised." Feet braced apart, hands jammed in my pockets, I faced Mom and Dr. Ferguson. I still thought of him as Dr. Ferguson even though he and my mom had been married nearly three months, and I was supposed to call him Ted.

"Lisa!" My mother cut in sharply. "I never promised you a horse. I said maybe we could get a horse after Ted and I got married." She smiled at him, "But we've decided to raise alpacas now. Starting a business like that is expensive. I'm afraid the horse will have to wait for a few years. Besides, you'll like the alpacas."

I stamped my foot. "A few years! I'll be grown up by then. I won't like alpacas. I'll hate them." I stopped for a moment. "What is an alpaca anyway?"

Dr. Ferguson grinned. "Lisa, isn't it a bit hasty to hate something when you don't even know what it is? "I do know," I blurted out. "I just remembered. They're a big ugly bird like an ostrich, aren't they?" I was sure that's what I'd seen in the school encyclopedia.

Dr. Ferguson winked at Mom. "Let's hope they can't fly over those fences we're putting up." Mom smiled and was about to say something, but stopped.

Yesterday, when I had come home from school, workmen had been enclosing one of our pastures with a closely knit wire fence. I'd thought it was just something to do with Dr. Ferguson's veterinary practice, which he was now running from the farm.

So much had changed around our place since Dr. Ferguson had married my mother. Some changes, I had to admit, were for the better. For one thing, we weren't always having to count our pennies to see if we could make it to the end of the month. Sometimes we even went out for dinner now. That was unheard of when Mom and I were on our own after Dad left. Mom worked at home now, helping Dr. Ferguson in his clinic. Even I had been given a job after school and on the week-ends, so I could earn some spending money.

But some changes were definitely for the worse. My mother acted like a teenager in love. It was embarrassing! I tried to keep my friends away. How do you explain grownups who are always holding hands and smiling at each other with googly eyes? The magic floating between them made me feel like an intruder. They hardly knew I existed anymore.

My cousin, Paul, thinks they're neat. He must be getting to the romantic stage too. Even though he's just my age, nearly twelve, he's suddenly started slicking his hair back with some sort of goo. He sure talks about girls a lot. Last week he asked Diane, another girl in our class, to a show. She wouldn't go though, because she'd just gotten braces and was scared she'd end up with popcorn stuck in them. That *would* be embarrassing!

I was sitting at the kitchen table, staring out the window and daydreaming as usual. I glanced at Mom and Dr. Ferguson out of the corner of my eye. They were at it again, their heads together, smiling and talking in low voices. Yes, I really didn't matter to Mom anymore, except when she needed to remind me of something.

She looked over at me. "Hurry up, Lisa, you'll be late for your baby-sitting course," she reminded me, as if reading my thoughts.

As I trudged slowly upstairs to get my jacket, my dog Roper trotted behind me, hopeful that a jacket for me meant a walk for him.

"Later, Roper," I promised, patting his head.

Ever since Tiffy, the big, gray, hairy cat, had arrived with Dr. Ferguson, Roper had been sticking to me like glue. One of Roper's favorite pastimes had been chasing cats—that is, until Tiffy arrived. Tiffy's favorite pastime was chasing dogs. After the first painful encounter left Roper's nose scratched, he'd stayed out of her way.

I sat on my bed, absently stroking the golden grasshopper on the chain around my neck. I always found a strange comfort in running my fingers over the glowing golden metal insect that Gagar had left me last year. Though its power had long since disappeared, the grasshopper held a lot of wonderful memories.

My other hand fondled one of Roper's silky ears. "You and I could have gone back to the planet Ylepithon with Gagar. Mom probably wouldn't even miss us."

Roper banged his tail on the floor, but I'm not so sure he really would have enjoyed going to Ylepithon with Gagar. Roper had suffered badly when Paul and I had used him as the chief food source for the fleas we had collected for Gagar.

That adventure had happened last summer, when Gagar, from the planet Ylepithon, had visited Paul and me one night when we were sleeping in our farmyard under the stars.

Gager had asked us to collect fleas for his

planet, where fleas were used to generate flying power. He had explained that Ylepithon's flea colonies were dying off. Then Gagar had given us the golden grasshopper to enable us to fly and promised that if we collected all the fleas he needed, he would re-charge the golden grasshopper for us permanently.

I should say "me". Paul never would try flying with the golden grasshopper. But my memories of flying with the golden grasshopper were wonderful, except for the last time, when the flea capacitor had abruptly run out of power. I had plummeted into a haystack a few kilometers away and had had to walk home in the dark.

"Li...sa," my mother's voice floated up through the heat register, our effective if old-fashioned intercom. "You're late! What's keeping you?" Then more insistently, "Have you done your chores?"

Omigosh, the chores! I'd forgotten all about them. Yanking my jacket out of the closet, I ran downstairs with Roper at my heels.

"I'll do the chores as soon as I get back. I'll be home by five o'clock," I promised, running for the door.

"Lisa!" Dr. Ferguson blocked the doorway. "I've just done my rounds. The dogs' water dishes are nearly empty. You haven't cleaned the cages. I'm paying you to do a responsible job, young lady, but animals must be looked after when they need it, not when it's convenient for you."

I tried to look contrite. "Okay, I'm sorry, I'm sorry, but I've got to go. This last night of our course is the test. I'll do it all when I get home at five."

"You and Paul were supposed to move the recycling bins on the weekend. You forgot about that too. The workmen are putting a fence through there tomorrow, Lisa, so they have to be moved tonight."

I groaned inwardly. I had at least two hours of homework as well. I was trying hard not to daydream in school this year. If I worked hard, I'd have good marks going into grade seven. It seemed I was an incurable daydreamer. But, if I couldn't daydream in school, then I had to have time to do it at home. Didn't grown-ups understand that?

"Oh yeah, I forgot. Okay, I'll do that too." I mustered a weak smile to show I would really try hard not to forget.

Dr. Ferguson glanced over my head at Mom. His look softened. He stepped aside as I latched my helmet over my head, jumped on my bike, and headed down the driveway.

"Li . . . sa," he called out with a sigh, "Roper's following you. You forgot to tie him up."

CHAPTER 2

I punched the pillow into a ball behind my head and switched on the reading lamp. This was my favorite time of the day. I could usually manage to read for a couple of hours after going to bed. Mom used to check on me in the past, but not any more.

Tonight I was tired, but pleased with myself. I'd missed only one question on the test for my baby-sitter certificate. I said the first thing you check when a baby cries is to see whether it's hungry. But the instructor said you're to check for an open diaper pin. I didn't know anyone still used diaper pins. Besides, I had no intention of baby-sitting anyone in diapers. Changing diapers is just not my idea of fun. I'd taken the course so that I could baby-sit our neighbor's little girl. Between that and working in the clinic, I could maybe save enough for a computer.

Paul had ridden over after the class to help me move the re-cycling bins. Then I'd done the chores and afterwards my two hours of homework. I'd even had time to take Roper for that promised walk.

I began to read my book. As I turned a page, a paw nudged my elbow which is Roper's way of saying, "Please, may I come up?"

I patted the bed. "Come on."

He leapt up and wiggled over me, giving me a slurp on the face in passing. Sniffing at the blankets, he pawed them and turned around slowly at least three times before snuggling down, his back against my leg. Why do dogs turn around so many times before they lie down? Someday I'm going to figure out the answer to that question.

After a few minutes of reading I began yawning. It had been a long day. Tomorrow was Saturday and I could read then. Turning my reading lamp off, I closed my eyes, my hand on Roper's back.

Have you ever been awakened by a dog snoring? My bedside clock glowed 3:00 a.m. I shoved Roper as he grunted and snuffled and twitched, no doubt dreaming of a battle with Tiffy. Realizing my bedroom ceiling light was still on, I sleepily stumbled to the door to switch it off.

The need to cross back to bed in the dark woke me up completely. Perhaps it's silly, but I've always imagined something living under my bed, lurking, just waiting to grab a foot. Normally, I take a flying leap from the middle of the room to land on top of the bed. That way, my feet can't be grabbed from under the bed.

I stopped, poised, in the middle of the darkened room. What if I landed on Roper and squashed him? I was tiptoeing towards the bed, when I heard a noise outside the window. With under-the-bed monster jitters in my brain, it's a wonder I didn't scream at the top of my lungs. But I didn't. . . for there was something vaguely familiar about the sound. The blind prevented me from seeing out.

"**Li...sa**," a mechanical voice chimed faintly through the window.

It couldn't be! I silently tiptoed to the window, listening. Roper whined uneasily in the dark.

"Sh...sh..." I whispered, "it's okay." I cautiously pulled the blind down to release the spring, then let it up a bit and peeked underneath.

Gagar! Just as I'd thought. In my excitement I let the blind go whirling to the top with a loud SNAP.

Gagar's squat little body looked as alien as ever with his large bald head and enormous, unblinking eyes, but I wasn't scared. He was an old friend. I tugged at the old window. Groaning, it finally slid upwards.

Something rustled behind me. Moonlight washed over the bed. Roper, who must have decided this whole scene wasn't for him, was belly-crawling under the blankets towards the foot of the bed. Only the tip of his tail stuck out. He stopped at the bottom, a quivering lump.

"It's okay, Roper," I whispered, "it's only Gagar from the planet Ylepithon. He won't hurt us."

Roper's tail moved once to acknowledge that he'd heard me, but he stayed where he was, secure under the blankets.

Forcing the window as high as it would go, I stuck my head out. Gagar was standing on the sloping red roof, his hands on his hips. Tangled wires led from what must have been his ears, along his arms and legs to the little box attached at his waist with a belt of racing colored lights. The softly glowing dome of the spaceship lit up the lawn below.

"I didn't think you'd ever come back. I'm sorry about the fleas last year—how they all got away and stuff."

The little box tinkled with laughter. **"Not a**

- 17 -

problem, not a problem. Sometimes when things don't work out, it's for the best, as this was."

"It was?" I asked. I'd been feeling kind of bad all year, thinking we'd let Gagar down.

"Yes, when our mission failed here, we decided to try another solar system. We found the planet Tular, where the fleas can jump a half a kilometre high. Imagine having that much power for our flea capacitors."

"Wow," I gasped, trying to imagine what such super fleas would do to Roper.

He chortled. **"They'd make mincemeat out of Roper, I'm afraid."**

I'd almost forgotten that Gagar could read my mind. Did he know everything about me, I wondered nervously? Did he read all my thoughts?

"No, I'm much too busy. I only pick up things that concern me," his box answered, the intrusion making me jump.

"Your flea capacitor quit on you prematurely. Let me see it please," Gagar's translator box blipped. I fumbled with the chain around my neck until the clasp came apart and handed the golden grasshopper to Gagar. He stared at it intently, turning it over and over in his hand.

"Just as I suspected. This flea capacitor was not made on Ylepithon. It is of inferior quality. Our

neighboring planet produces cheap imitations. Somehow this one got mixed in with ours." He chuckled. **"You were lucky to land in a haystack.**

"I will replace this with our new, improved version which my mate is designing at present, and you will truly be able to fly for the rest of your life."

I put my hand out. "No, I . . . I think I just want to keep this one to remind me of the wonderful flights I had last year."

Gagar dropped the golden grasshopper in my hand. **"But I thought you wished to fly."**

"I did. . . I do. . . but. . . but. . . I'm getting too old for it."

Gagar stared at me for a moment. **"You mean you don't want to be different from the other kids."**

"No, I don't mind being different—but that's being a whole lot different. How many kids do you know who can fly around in the air?"

Gagar chuckled. **"Well, they all do where I come from—once they earn their flea capacitor. But yes, here on earth, I see what you mean."**

"Besides, I had to be so careful not to be seen. The braver I got, the further I went. Who knows when I might have been picked up by radar and shot down by a missile or something."

I put the chain around my neck again and caressed the golden grasshopper. "I'll just keep it for the memories. It's like an old friend."

"**Well, now you've put a rat in my teeth**," Gagar said in exasperation.

"Pardon?" I asked, looking closely at him to see what he meant.

"**That's an old Ylepithon saying—from a time when we had teeth. It means you've put an obstacle in my path. I have a problem I was hoping you would help me with, but now I have nothing to offer in return.**"

"Another problem?" I asked, becoming a little annoyed. *Now* what did he want me to collect.

Gagar's voice tinkled with laughter as he once again read my mind. "**No, no...I do not want you to collect anything. This time, I have brought my daughter, Galena, for you to baby-sit!**"

CHAPTER 3

I must have still been feeling guilty about letting Gagar down last summer, or maybe I was feeling full of confidence after my baby-sitting course, or . . . maybe my brain was turning to mush. Whatever the reason, I'd somehow agreed, and now a little creature in a purple space suit stood staring at me with enormous, unblinking black eyes. One of her hands tightly clasped Gagar's, the other clutched a little furry object. Gagar's other hand held a small silver suitcase. What had I gotten myself into now?

The colored lights on the little creature's belt blinked and raced in different tracks. When hers stopped, Gagar's did too.

Gagar's voice tinkled with laughter. **"Galena says you look weird, Lisa. It's the first time she's met a real humanoid."**

I looked weird! Except for a mass of long golden curls, and the fact that she was less than half his size, she looked exactly like Gagar. And she thought *I* looked weird?

"I don't understand," I said, perplexed. "Why do you want me to baby-sit her?"

"Galena is developing a unique power and is meant for great things in the future of Ylepithon. As you know, we lived on Earth many millennia ago. It is very important for her to get in touch with her roots, as your saying goes." He stepped forward, pulling Galena along with him. **"Besides, I'm on my way to Tular to get a shipment of their wonderful fleas. I took Galena the last time. She thought the fleas were cute and let them out of their cage. They leapt around the spaceship with such force that it threw us off course and we were much delayed getting home."**

"What about her mother?" I asked.

"My Mate is of super intelligence and is very busy designing the new flea capacitor to handle the power of these monsters. She has no time for Galena at present," Gagar replied, prying his hand loose from Galena's in order to gesture as he spoke.

"She must love her a lot. She will miss her," I persisted.

The lights on both of their belts went out for a few seconds as they regarded each other in silence. Gagar turned back to me. Then the lights on his belt danced again.

"Love? I had forgotten about that ancient

emotion. **In order to survive, it is said our beings left that behind when they left Earth.**" He looked at Galena for a moment and then back at me. "**Let me think . . . love . . . mmm . . . It's not the same as fear, or anger, is it?**"

I shook my head, for once at a loss for words.

"**How about embarrassment, is it similar to that feeling?**" he asked, somewhat perplexed. I shook my head again.

"**Ah . . . ha . . . There is another emotion we feel. Tolerance. I think that might be close. But love? No, we do not experience it.**" He scratched his chin. "**Do you find it useful?**"

"Love? Useful? Well, I . . . I . . ." Again I found myself unable to elaborate. How could you explain love in terms of usefulness, especially to someone who had never experienced it?

In the background, the spaceship made a whirling sound and glowed brightly.

"**I must be off.**" He thrust the silver suitcase at me.

"But, wait, I know nothing about Galena. How am I supposed to look after her?"

"**Inside the suitcase, there are instructions and a few things you'll need. Galena is used to spending a great deal of time by herself. Besides, her only mission here is to get an education. She won't be a lot of trouble.**"

"But . . . but how long is this for anyway? Will you be back tomorrow?"

Gagar didn't look at me. **"Our time is very different than yours. Not tomorrow, but soon,"** he said vaguely.

He turned to Galena, holding his hand up with fingers spread apart. She did the same and their hands met briefly.

"By the way, Lisa, alpacas were part of our ancient past. They were thought to be very precious, as they are today. Galena will 'tolerate' them, I'm sure, and you might, as you say, 'love' them."

"Love a big, ugly bird?" I scoffed.

Gagar just laughed his tinkling laugh as, stroking his flea capacitor, he gently floated up into the air and over the side of the house. Moments later, the spaceship lifted off in a blaze of humming light. It disappeared before my very eyes.

Galena walked to the window and shyly put her hand up to me. She was too short to climb over the window sill. I leaned out and put my arms out to lift her. She quickly took a step backward with her hand still up, then she spread the fingers of her hand toward me, as she had done to Gagar. I did the same back and our hands touched briefly. Then she stepped forward, allowing herself to be lifted over the sill.

I expected her to be heavy and warm like a small child, but her body was cool to the touch. She wasn't any heavier than a stuffed doll, but I soon learned she really was alive!

Roper must have begun to suffocate under all the blankets. He crawled out and jumped off the bed. Sniffing the air, he took a step towards Galena.

"Yikes!" her translator box yelped. She scrambled up my legs and wrapped herself around my waist from behind. With her arms around my neck, she clung to me in a strangle hold.

"Ouch! Galena, your translator box is digging into my back." Gently pulling her hands apart so I could breathe, I commanded Roper to "Stay!" He sat down, thumping his tail.

Galena relaxed. Pulling her around, I sat her on the bed. "See, Galena, Roper won't hurt you. You've never seen a dog before, have you? He's a dog. D-o-g. Dog." I muttered. What else hadn't Gagar told me?

"Dog. D-o-g. Dog?" Galena's translator box chimed in a singsong voice.

I sighed. "No, just dog. He's a dog. His name is Roper."

"Roper Dog." Galena said, putting out her little

hand. Roper slowly approached her, sniffing her outstretched hand. His tail began to wag. Galena tinkled with laughter.

"Well, it looks as if she's learned to 'tolerate' you pretty quickly," I said to Roper as he lay down beside the bed.

I suddenly felt exhausted and realized my head hurt. Too much had happened tonight. The clock said 4:30 a.m. I had to get to bed. Galena was beginning to droop as well.

Where was she supposed to sleep? I briefly considered my closet, but there was too much junk on the floor. Besides, it was her first night here. I couldn't really just dump her in the closet, could I?

I threw the bedcovers back further. "Just for tonight, okay? Just for tonight, you get to sleep with me." As I picked her up, she began to look frantically around the room.

"Tedu." she chimed.

"Tedu? What's a Tedu?" I asked. I was too tired for this. I tried to put her down, but she kicked and fussed. Then I remembered the little furry thing she'd had in her hand when I first saw her. Carrying her over to the window, we found it behind the suitcase, where she must have dropped it when I lifted her through the window.

She grabbed it and clasped it to her chest.

"Tedu." her voice box crooned.

Since the moon had disappeared, I had to feel my way with my feet. No use worrying about monsters under the bed any more, I had an alien in my arms! I laid her in the middle of the bed, climbed in beside her and pulled the blankets up to our chins.

My head still spun. Tomorrow, I was going to have to figure all this out, but for now... I yawned.

A paw reached over the side of the bed and gently swiped at my nose. I sighed. There was probably enough room for all three of us.

"Come on," I said, patting the bed.

CHAPTER 4

Instructions for Galena

1. *Change nourishment bands as needed. Make sure Galena utilizes the vegetables as well as the desserts.*
2. *Galena must spend most of her time with the IDs. These are disks containing all of Earth's history and information to the present day. This is her education about Earth. Make sure she uses all of them, as she may prefer some over others.*

I rooted through the little suitcase. That was it for instructions? I'd expected there would be a whole manual of instructions—at least as many as you get with a Nintendo game! It was eight o'clock, time for my morning chores. Mom might check at any moment to see why I hadn't come downstairs yet.

All the suitcase contained was the piece of paper with the instructions, two small boxes, and three more purple space suits.

Galena perched on the edge of the bed watching me, Tedu still clutched in her hand. Roper sniffed at one of the boxes in the suitcase. I picked it up. *Nourishment Bands* was printed on the outside. Inside were several wide band-aid like strips with rows of colored bumps. Many bumps were in shades of green, the rest were white, red, orange, brown, yellow, purple and even black. There were also a couple of bumps that had weird colours I couldn't name. On the bottom of the box it said: "Warning: not for humanoid use".

Fat chance I'd ever try them, I thought to myself, wrinkling up my nose.

"I can't believe it smells like food to you, Roper. I bet it's not even close to food as we know it," I commented as he sniffed at the bands.

I looked up at Galena. "Do you need one of these now?"

She shook her head and held out her wrist. I pulled back the edge of her sleeve. The band she had on was almost full of bumps. She pressed a white, and then a brown and yellow bump.

"I hope that was a wise choice for breakfast," I muttered to myself, sitting down beside her.

"I have to go, Galena. I don't know how I'm going to explain to people what you are and why you're here. You're going to have to stay up here and be very quiet while I do the chores and think of something. Do you understand?"

Galena nodded as she climbed down off the bed and got the box of IDs from her suitcase. She turned it upside down on the bed. Hundreds of tiny gold coloured disks about the size of a dime fluttered out. I picked one up to examine.

"*The Fall of the Roman Empire*!" I picked up another. "*The History of the Nuclear Age*!" I read in disbelief. What kind of super kid was this anyway!

Solemnly, Galena took one of the disks from me and climbed back up on the bed. She propped herself against the wall, popped open a little compartment on the side of her translator box, inserted the disk and pushed a button. As the coloured lights blinked on her belt, she became motionless, as if in a trance. I waved a hand in front of her eyes, but she didn't respond.

"Maybe it's like virtual reality," I said to Roper, who eyed her with interest. "You know, it's as if you're experiencing the whole thing. She's certainly tuned into something."

Roper just looked at me without wagging his tail. I guess he just understands "dog" things like "walk", "dinner", "cat"—stuff that really means something to him—but not "virtual reality".

"Come on, Roper, we've got to go," I said, opening my door. But Roper wouldn't come. He whined, looking back at Galena, and then lay down on the floor beside the bed.

"You want to baby-sit? Okay, good dog. I'll be back soon," I said, patting him on the head.

CHAPTER 5

"Get over here! I don't care if you were planning on biking with Diane," I whispered urgently to Paul on the phone. Cupping my hand around the mouthpiece, I lowered my voice even further. "Gagar came back Friday night. You won't believe what he wants me to do this time!" I chewed on my thumbnail. "Besides, I need your help."

Paul hadn't been home all day yesterday. I had spent the day itching to share the news of Galena's arrival with him.

Galena hadn't been any trouble. In fact she'd just sat in my room all day immersing herself in different IDs: *Demise of the Dinosaurs, The Second World War, The Industrial Revolution.* She wasn't even using the disks in the proper historical order. I don't know what kind of a jumbled up pile of knowledge she was absorbing about the Earth, but she was learning more than I'd know in a zillion years.

I really did need Paul's help. Not with Galena.

I needed his advice about something else.

Michael Black was a boy in our grade 6 class. He and I had a "thing" going for each other that had started last year. We often did our homework together and we'd gone to a few shows. I'd worn skirts more often this past year, because Michael told me they looked nice. We'd even experimented with a few kisses. I wasn't sure I liked kissing, but maybe I'd develop a taste for it.

Lately, however, he'd been different—almost as if he were changing his mind about liking me. Boys talk to other boys about boy things. Maybe Paul knew something.

Dr. Ferguson stuck his head inside the door just as I hung up the phone. "Oh good. You're here. I need your help for a little while."

"But Paul's on his way over. Can't we do it later?"

"No, I need you now. Your mother is out picking cherries, and Mr. Johnson just dropped his dog off. Mitsy's had a run in with a raccoon. I'd like you to hold her while I suture a couple of wounds."

"Oh, all right." I tried not to let on how pleased I was. Usually Mom helped with all the neat stuff and I just did the cleaning and feeding. I followed him out to what had been our garage, but which was now renovated into a clinic.

Mitsy was feeling very sorry for herself. She cowered in the corner of her box, shaking. She wasn't hurt too badly, just a small gash on the back of her neck and another on her paw. Dr. Ferguson felt the wounds would heal more quickly if they were stitched. As well, he would give her a shot of antibiotics to prevent infection.

"Just hold her gently, but very firmly, Lisa," he cautioned me as he swabbed the cuts with antiseptic. "This won't hurt much, but she's scared."

Holding her, I watched, fascinated, as he deftly stitched the wound together, all the while talking softly to Mitsy.

"Good dog," he said. "Hold still one more second. A shot . . . and you're all finished."

I put my face down close to hers. "That wasn't so bad was it, Mitsy?" With a growl, she bared her teeth and bit me on the nose.

"Owww!" I yelled, letting go. She fled to her box in the corner, where she once again huddled in a ball, watching me clutch my nose.

Dr. Ferguson was at my side instantly. He pulled my hand away. "Let's have a look." He frowned, then went for the bottle of antiseptic.

"You have a couple of skin punctures. You'll need a tetanus shot later."

"Yuck! I hate shots!"

Dr. Ferguson chuckled. "So does Mitsy, obviously." He frowned again as he dabbed the antiseptic on, while I winced at the sting.

"Lisa, never ever . . ."

"I know, I know," I interrupted. "Never ever put your face down near an animal when it's scared or in pain. I just wasn't thinking," I said.

"You were thinking about the animal rather than yourself," he said with a small smile.

"Lisa?" Paul's voice floated in through the window.

"I'm in here," I hollered.

Dr. Ferguson winced. "Lisa, please go to the door instead of shouting. We want to heal the animals here, not traumatize them further."

"Oh, sorry." I headed out the door.

"What happened to you?" I could tell by the look on his face that mine looked pretty weird.

"Come on, I'll tell you on the way. Mom will probably be home soon. I want you to meet someone," I urged, running ahead.

CHAPTER 6

O h wow, is she for real?" Paul's stared wide-eyed at Galena, who was perched in her usual spot on the bed. I'd told him all about her on the way upstairs.

"She's for real all right," I said, frowning. "I think she's immersed in the *Exploration of North America* right now. At least, that's the ID she showed me this morning."

"Galena." I waved my hand in front of her face, but she didn't acknowledge me. Leaning over, I pushed the stop button on her translator box. She looked up at me and then at Paul.

"Yikes!" she blipped. She was about to scramble to me for safety, when I put my hand down to stop her.

"It's okay, Galena. This is my cousin, Paul. He's also a friend."

Galena's big black eyes fixed on Paul. "Friend? What is a friend?"

"Omigosh, you don't know what a friend is

either? Well... a friend is... a friend is someone you like to spend time with."

Her face remained blank and I realized that if she spent most of her time by herself in her world as well as mine, then it was no wonder she didn't know what a friend was.

Suddenly, Roper pushed his head between Paul and me, his tail slapping both our legs. He panted happily as he shoved his wet nose against Galena's hand.

Absently, Paul and I both stroked his back, while Galena stroked his head. Being the sappy dog that he is, Roper was in his glory. His tail beat even harder as he rested his head on Galena's lap.

"See, Roper is your friend," I explained. "He's my friend, too."

"And mine, too," said Paul, giving him a final pat. "Aren't you, boy? Sit. Shake a paw," he commanded. Galena's voice box tinkled with laughter as Roper obeyed.

"I understand now. Roper is my friend too," Galena said. She looked up at me. "Are you my friend too, Lisa?" she asked in her musical voice.

"Well... I guess I am." I hadn't spent much time with Galena. I wasn't sure I wanted to when she was immersed in IDs all the time—so being her friend really didn't fit my definition. But maybe she had her own idea now about what a friend was ... and maybe, for some strange reason, I fit it.

Taking her small hand, I squeezed it. "Yes, I'm your friend," I said smiling.

"Do you know of a Christopher Columbus?" asked Galena, changing the subject completely.

"Christopher Columbus! Of course we know of him," Paul and I chimed together.

In fourteen hundred and ninety-two.
Columbus sailed the ocean blue,

Miss Smith, our grade 5 social studies teacher, had made sure that we knew all about every boring explorer that had ever landed in North or South America.

"He's a very interesting fellow. This ID puts me on his ship, the Santa Maria. There's a storm coming up. I must go back." Galena propped herself back up against the wall. Looking up at Paul, she raised her hand with fingers spread apart. He looked at me and shrugged.

"Just do it back," I said. "It's her way of greeting and saying good-bye."

Paul spread his fingers and touched her hand. Galena hit the play button. Immediately, she withdrew into herself and was no longer with us.

"What a weird kid!" Paul said, staring at her. He picked up her box of IDs, looking at the ones she'd already used and filed neatly in the cover. His eyes grew wide. "You mean she knows all this stuff, just by doing this?" He waved his hand at Galena. "Wow! What a way to learn! I wonder if her translator box would work for me. Maybe there's an ID in there that says *Grade Six*."

"Fat chance of that. She's learned more since she arrived here than you or I will probably learn in our lifetimes. Grade six would take her about two seconds." I wrinkled my nose. "I wouldn't want to learn that way. She looks like a zombie."

Roper woofed and ran to the window as a car drove into the driveway. Mom was back with the cherries. Any minute she'd be calling me to help her.

"Paul," I had to ask now, "what's going on with Michael?"

His eyes slid away, as he headed for the door. "What do you mean?"

I followed him out. Suddenly I was relieved to be talking to his back. "Well, he's different lately. I know guys talk. Doesn't he like me any more?"

Paul didn't reply. He headed downstairs, with Roper and me on his heels.

"I told Galena that you were my friend, Paul. If that's true, you'll tell me." I said sharply.

He turned so quickly that Roper and I nearly piled into him. "Maybe the reason I'm not telling you is because I *am* your friend," he offered.

CHAPTER 7

H urry up, Lisa. You'll miss the bus," Mom's voice floated up the air register intercom.

"Yeah, yeah, I know. My hair won't stay put and my face is a mess," I muttered, dabbing at the red marks on my nose with some liquid make-up. Glancing at my watch and checking my reflection in the mirror, I shouted down the air register, "Co...ming."

It must be going to rain, I thought. The Okanagan Valley, where we live, is so dry that my long, red curly hair is usually fairly manageable. But today, no sooner did I tie it back in a pony tail, then SPROING, all these fuzzy, wispy bits escaped. That only happened before a rain. Smoothing them once more with wet hands, I ran for the door. After a quick look to check on Galena, I grabbed my school books and ran downstairs with Roper at my heels.

Mom was already at work canning cherries. The lid of the canner on the stove chattered and danced as the steam tried to escape. Dr.

Ferguson's cat, Tiffy, was curled up in her usual spot—on his chair—watching everything with green, menacing eyes. As Roper followed me into the kitchen, she stared at him, her tail twitching back and forth. Roper took one look, froze in his tracks, then slunk to the door with his tail between his legs. I quickly let him out.

After Paul's visit the night before, Mom had taken me to the walk-in clinic for a tetanus shot. After we had gotten home, I'd washed and pitted cherries until I felt like a cherry. Usually I would have grumbled, but after Paul's reaction to my question about Michael, I was glad for a chore to distract me.

"Don't forget, the alpacas are arriving tonight." Mom handed me the milk and sat down at the table. "Ted is already down at the barn getting things ready. I'm glad I'm nearly finished with the cherries." Sighing, she pushed a strand of hair out of her eyes.

What with Gagar and Galena on my mind, I had quite forgotten that the alpacas were arriving tonight—not that it really mattered. They'd probably just mean more work for me.

"I was going to Paul's to do homework after school," I said.

Mom smiled. "That's okay, it'll be a surprise for when you get home."

"Yeah, right," I said, frowning. I grabbed the last piece of toast and my lunch bag off the counter.

"I see the bus. I've got to go." I turned at the door to look at her. "Mom, are you okay? You look awfully tired."

A small smile played at Mom's lips. "I'm fine. I'll have a little nap later. Now hurry up, or you'll be walking to school."

I sat in my usual spot on the bus beside Paul. He'd obviously spent the night thinking about Galena and how she was learning so much by using the IDs.

"What disk was she learning from today?" Paul asked eagerly into my ear. Not that he had to be careful. There was so much noise on our bus that he could have probably shouted at the top of his lungs and no one would have paid attention.

"I don't know," I said as another wisp of hair SPROINGED its escape from my ponytail. "I didn't have time to look." Pushing the annoying bit of hair behind my ear, I looked Paul directly in the eyes. "Come on, tell me about Michael!"

At the mention of Michael's name, Paul abruptly looked out the window, leaving me staring at the back of his head. When I craned forward to look at his face, I could tell from the line of his jaw, he wasn't going to tell me anything. Thoroughly annoyed, I tried to concentrate on a book for the rest of the trip. Boys could be such a pain!

When I rushed off the bus to catch up with Diane, Paul called my name from somewhere behind, but I decided to let him know what it felt like to be ignored.

All through math period I tried to make eye contact with Michael, but he seemed to be intent on avoiding me. He glanced my way once, but when he caught me looking at him, he quickly looked away. When the period was three quarters over, I was still on question one of the assignment. If I didn't want tons of homework, I'd better get moving, I told myself. Michael would have to be dealt with at lunchtime.

Second period, Monday morning is my favorite class of the week, because it's usually creative writing. Today though, Mr. Thomas had a project in mind.

"Since you'll be going on to grade 7 soon..." Mr. Thomas leaned forward onto Brad Summer's desk, the sun reflecting off his bald head. He looked out at all of us. "At least, I hope you will be—ha, ha, ha..."

"Ha, ha, ha," we all laughed back. Mr. Thomas was always making these dumb jokes and we'd soon learned it was better to laugh; otherwise he'd just keep making them until we did.

Mr. Thomas straightened up. "It's time you started learning how to manage your own time." He turned towards the blackboard. "This assignment will be independently done over a period of two weeks. Here are the criteria." He began writing.

Friendship Booklet

- write one poem pertaining to friendship (does not have to rhyme) 20
- make a labelled poster to show various things friends can do together.............20
- make a list of the attributes of a good friend...10
- write a story with friendship as the theme...10
- oral presentation.............................10

There were moans and groans as people quickly scribbled down the criteria. But the project didn't look too bad to me—most of it could be treated as creative writing. I also liked making things. If I had had a computer already, it would all have been a lot easier.

As I passed Brad Summer's desk on my way to the pencil sharpener, Brad stuck out his foot. I'll never know if he did it on purpose or not. Naturally, being a klutzy person, I tripped and did a jerky hop, skip and jump to keep myself from landing headfirst on the floor. I turned to confront Brad, but he ignored me, distress written all over his face.

You have to know Brad Summers and our history of dislike for each other in order to understand why he might have tripped me on purpose. It started last year when he filched my golden grasshopper one day and wouldn't give it back. A bit later we got into a cake fight over a bottle of fleas. The guy's been a loser ever since he moved here at the beginning of last year. Nobody really likes him because he is always trying to bug people. His nickname is "Wormface". That says it all!

Anyway, he looked pretty upset and hadn't even noticed that I'd just about killed myself tripping over his big foot, so I kept my nasty remarks to myself and sharpened my pencil.

Out of the corner of my eye, I saw Brad leave his desk to approach Mr. Thomas.

"I can't do the assignment," he said.

Mr. Thomas looked up at Brad, clearly annoyed.

"Pardon?" he demanded in a rather threatening voice.

Brad stood his ground. "I ... I can't do the assignment," he repeated.

Mr. Thomas glared at Brad. "What do you mean you can't do the assignment? Why can't you do the assignment?" Mr. Thomas's voice dripped with sarcasm. I guess he thought he'd heard every excuse there was for not doing an assignment.

Brad shifted from one foot to the other. He looked at the floor, his face all red.

"I can't do any of this stuff, because ... I've never had a friend."

By this time my pencil was as sharp as a needle. I returned to my desk, trying not to let on that I'd heard the exchange.

He had to be telling a lie, didn't he? Galena was the only other being I knew who'd never had a friend, but she was from a different planet where the word "friend" wasn't even known. As I said earlier, no one really liked Brad Summers, but how could a guy go through life for twelve years without ever having a single friend?

I didn't really have a lot of friends, either. There was Paul—even though just then I was mad at him, and there was Michael—although just then I wasn't sure what was going on with him. There were a couple of girls in class who could probably be called friends. And there was always Roper. Everyone has to have had at least one friend though, right?

Then I remembered something else that had happened a week earlier. Mr. Thomas had been in one of his rare good moods. He had a roll of masking tape in his hand as he stood at the door, dismissing us for lunch. As each of us went by, he tore off a strip of tape and stuck it somewhere on our face, saying, "You're special."

Most of us had giggled or groaned, as we tore it off to stick it back on Mr. Thomas, or someone else who was nearby. But not Brad. He put his hand over the piece of tape and ran out. During the lunch hour, I heard a first grader ask him why he had a piece of tape stuck to his cheek. Brad told the kid, " 'Cause I'm special."

When he came back in after lunch, he still had the tape on. In fact, he wore it for the rest of the day. A couple of times I noticed him absently stroking the tape with his finger, a faraway look in his eyes. He was one weird kid!

I jumped at the lunch bell—caught daydreaming again. Surely, there were better things to daydream about than Wormface Brad Summers. I'd even missed how he and Mr. Thomas had resolved the problem with the assignment. Brad still looked glum and Mr.

Thomas growled a bit when he dismissed us, so they must still be at odds.

Grabbing my lunch bag, I hurried out the door, watching Michael's blond head as he loped across the field. I figured I'd catch him alone just as he left the school yard to go home for lunch.

"Michael," I shouted, running to catch up.

When he saw me, a funny look came across his face. I stopped short in front of him, panting from the run.

"Hi," I said, not knowing what else to say.

"Hi," Michael said, looking past me. He shifted uncomfortably. "I got to get going or I won't be back in time for the bell." He turned away.

"Wait a minute. I want to know what's going on between us," I half hollered to his back. My hands went to my hips in the defensive stance I take whenever I'm really annoyed with someone. "You've been ignoring me. I thought we were . . . well, I thought we were . . . you know . . ." My voice trailed off. When he looked back at me, I knew we were no longer whatever we'd been.

Michael tossed his blond head back and looked past me again. "I've changed my mind, Lisa. It's over!"

"It's over? But . . . but what did I do?" I could feel the blood draining out of my face.

"You didn't do anything. It's just...it's just your hair."

"My hair?" Grabbing my ponytail, I pulled the end of it around in front of me, staring dumbly at it. "My hair?" I asked again, not understanding.

"Yeah, your red hair. My dad says to beware of women with red hair. He said redheads have real tempers. I think it's true, too. My Aunt Hilda has red hair. She's always losing her temper at my dad—and he's her brother!"

Michael looked at me squarely in the face for the first time. "Besides, look at you. You're a mess! Did you comb your hair this morning? And what happened to your nose?"

Suddenly the blood was rushing back into my face. He was right. I was about to lose my temper!

"So, who do you think you are, some special Prince Charming?" I shouted. "You're nothing but vain...and shallow...and contemptible." I stopped to get my breath. "And I hope your Aunt Hilda takes a round out of your dad every time she sees him, because he's nothing but an old fart!"

Turning on my heel, I marched away, my head held high. But before I'd gone far, tears were streaming down my face.

I couldn't go back into the school looking like

this and soon the kids would all be out after finishing their lunches. I turned blindly towards the row of tall bushes at the schoolground's boundary.

In grade two I'd discovered a little hollow between two of the bushes, hidden by branches and leaves. Many lunch hours I used to crawl in there when no one was looking. I would lie on my back, with my head cradled in my arms and watch the sunlight and shadows dance through the leaves. It was a nest built for daydreaming. Sometimes when the bell rang, I could hardly remember where I really was.

I hadn't been there for a long time, not since grade three when I had discovered that I could just as easily daydream in class. Now I remembered that haven.

I had grown since grade three, but on my hands and knees I was able to squeeze in between two lower branches, where I crouched, sobbing.

It wasn't like I was in love with Michael. Not really. I wouldn't cry over any boy! What bothered me was the idea that a bad temper was connected to red hair.

My tears turned into hiccups. My hair wasn't really red, it was auburn. Often enough I had received comments about my pretty auburn hair from my mother's friends. Michael needed to learn the difference between auburn and red!

I had some money already saved for my computer, but suddenly this red hair business seemed more important. I had to show him he didn't know beans about what red hair really looked like. I'd show him what red really was!

Peering glumly through the lacy green curtain, I watched the kids in the playground. I saw Paul turning every which way, his hand shading his eyes. He must have guessed that I'd gone after Michael and he was looking for me. I knew he'd never find me on his own.

When I called to him, he followed my voice until, on hands and knees, he was peering in through the bushes at me.

"What are you doing, Lisa?" He took one look at my face, which by now must have been puffy and blotched from crying. "You've seen Michael."

"Yes." The tears threatened to overflow again. I gulped to hold them back. "Yes ... he's ... he's despicable." I spit the word out. Somehow the ring of it made me feel slightly better.

I held out my ponytail to Paul. "Is my hair really red?"

Paul looked at my hair and frowned. "Yeah, I guess it is."

"And, do I have a hot temper?" I demanded.

"Well, sometimes you do." Paul chuckled. "Remember when you dumped the cake on Brad Summers' head?"

"Do you think it's true that they're related, the red hair and the bad temper?"

Paul just looked at me. "Well...I don't know."

My ears started burning. "It can't be true, because my hair isn't really red. Neither one of you know what red hair's truly like!" I looked away, dismissing him. The bell rang.

"I'm not going back to class so don't try and talk me into it."

"Come on, Lisa. You'll get in trouble."

I waved my hand at him. "I don't care. I'm not going back looking like this. Tell the teacher my mom picked me up and I'm bringing a note tomorrow. Good-bye!" I pulled the branches together to block his view.

"I think you're more stubborn than hot headed. Maybe stubbornness comes with red hair," Paul muttered as he turned to leave.

"You think this is red, you wait till tomorrow," I shouted out of the bush, but I don't think he heard me. He was running towards the school, afraid of a detention for being late.

CHAPTER 8

The new me stepped off the public bus and started walking along the lane to our farm. I hoped I'd reach the house before the black clouds looming in the west got overhead. My hand crept up to my hair for what must have been the tenth time. It felt like a bristle brush.

I hadn't really meant to take such drastic measures, but sitting in that bush all afternoon waiting for school to be over had made me madder and madder at the injustice of the whole thing.

By the time I reached the hairdresser's after withdrawing my savings from the bank, I had decided to have my hair cut as well as coloured. When she asked how short, I told her very short! Then we chose the brightest red available. For added effect, even though the hairdresser thought it might be a bit much, I bought a can of henna-red mousse, which she worked into short spikes all over my head.

At least Mom would notice me now. I wasn't

too sure how she would react, but since she's always encouraging me to think for myself, this was proof that I could!

The back door was locked. Although it was close to five thirty, no one was home except Tiffy. Didn't that cat do anything but guard Dr. Ferguson's chair? I dropped my bag inside the door. Maybe someone was down at the barn.

Unlatching the barnyard gate, I could hear strange humming noises—not people humming, animals humming. I broke into a run, not knowing what to expect. Rounding the corner into the barn, I stopped short and gasped in amazement.

In the barn stood the most adorable looking creatures I'd ever seen . . . and they weren't birds. I'd forgotten all about the alpacas. Could these be alpacas? The long necks and fluffy bodies made them look like a cross between a giraffe and a puff ball. Gingerly, on dainty feet, they edged toward me, with ears pricked forward and large, black, curious eyes on the alert.

Suddenly, two baby heads, one black and one white, popped out of the furry mass. With soft short humming sounds, they crept forward, stretching their necks out to sniff my hair and face. A wet nose touched mine. I laughed. Putting my arms around the black one's neck to hug it was like embracing a pile of soft dandelion fluff. Abruptly, the black fluff pulled out of my grasp and whirled away, bucking and kicking, to the safety of its mom.

"Oh . . . " was all I could say.

I was in love!

"I see you've found them." Startled, I turned around to find Dr. Ferguson smiling at me. Mom wasn't far behind. Walking through the barn door, she took one look at me and stopped dead.

"Lisa, what on earth have you done to your hair?"

Forcing a nervous grin, I faced her. "Well, you encourage me to think independently. That's what I did."

Dr. Ferguson looked at me, a small smile playing at the corners of his mouth. "But did you plan on looking like a crimson hedgehog?"

I knew he was teasing.

"Yes, it's my new look!" I said firmly.

Mom was still frowning. It's the longest she'd looked at me in some time.

"But your beautiful long auburn hair. . . It looked so nice."

"Some people thought it was red. It wasn't red. This is. I'm just showing them what red is really like. Don't worry, it will grow out."

"Yes, in about six months." Mom sighed,

rolling her eyes. Dr. Ferguson gave her a look which said, "Just ignore it. It's a stage."

She took one last look at me. "Well, I'd better get dinner started."

The black baby approached me again. I put my hand out to be sniffed.

"What do you think, Lisa? Shall we keep them?"

"They're all adorable, but the babies are the cutest! Can this one be mine? Please!"

Dr. Ferguson laughed at the pleading in my voice. It wasn't often I pleaded with anyone.

"First of all Lisa, an alpaca baby is called a cria. I'm afraid it's just not possible for you to have your own cria. They're very valuable and will have to be sold as soon as they're grown up and bred."

My face must have shown my disappointment.

"You can, however, help look after them and work with all the alpacas, including the crias. They need lots of handling so they're used to human contact when they grow up."

"What do you mean?" I asked.

"Well, basically, they're a herd animal and would rather be left to themselves. Their legs are very precious, because running away from an enemy is their only defense. If we get them used to our touch, they will learn to trust us and it will be a lot easier to shear them and show them, and to help care for them when they're sick."

He cut open a bale of hay and handed me a flake.

"Put about this much in each feeder. That way, they'll get to know you." He leaned against the wall. "We'll give them a day or two to settle in before we start working with them. Next week someone will be coming over to shear some of them."

"Shear them?" I was horrified. "Why? They're so soft and beautiful the way they are."

"That's one of the reasons they're valuable. The fibre—that's what it's called—is one of the finest in the world. We can sell it for a good price. Besides, they need to be shorn to avoid heat stress. They're native to high mountain ranges in South America where it's much colder. Their coats have eight times the insulation of wool. How would you like to wear a coat like that on a hot summer day?"

"I guess that makes sense," I agreed, dropping hay in the last feeder.

"The animals are calm around you. You have good animal sense, Lisa." He glanced at my nose. "Well, most of the time."

It wasn't often Dr. Ferguson gave out compliments, to me at least. It made me glow inside.

"Maybe some day . . . "

A clap of thunder drowned the rest of his words. Within seconds, rain drummed furiously on the barn's metal roof. The animals milled around nervously at the unfamiliar din.

A flash of light filled the barn door, followed by another deafening crash of thunder. Through the door I could see a sky full of rolling, black clouds. Clearly, this was not just a shower.

"Come on, we'd better make a run for it." Dr. Ferguson yelled.

The rain pelted down, soaking us to the skin as we ran to the house. Roper, who had been waiting for us at the gate, beat a hasty retreat to the shelter of the veranda. He shook himself just as we walked by.

"Yuck, Roper. We don't need to be any wetter," I complained, stopping to take off my shoes.

Dr. Ferguson looked at me and began laughing. "Lisa, you'd better go look in the mirror!"

It was a good thing Mom's back was towards me as I ran through the kitchen and upstairs to the bathroom. She might have thought I was mortally wounded if she'd seen me. My face and neck were streaked with red where the mousse had washed off my hair. It had also bled into the neck of my white T-shirt.

Yanking off the soggy T-shirt, I splashed some water on my neck and face to rinse off the red streaks. To no effect. I scrubbed hard with a wash cloth, but they still remained. In desperation, I peeled off my clothes and soaped my face and neck vigorously during a long hot shower.

I wrapped the towel around me and combed what little hair I had left. I didn't put any more mousse in. The streaks had disappeared from my face and neck, but they were replaced by blotchy marks from all the scrubbing.

When I opened the door to my bedroom, Galena was at the window watching the storm.

"Yikes," she yelped when she saw me. "Who ate your hair?"

"No one ate my hair. I had it cut."

She just looked at me. "Cut?"

Galena may have been well informed about Earth's history, but she seemed a bit short on practical knowledge.

"Yes, cut—with scissors. Here, I'll show you."

Rooting around on top of my dresser, I found a pair of nail scissors. There wasn't much of my hair left to cut, and Roper was still outside on the veranda. I looked at Galena's long golden curls. Surely, one would never be missed.

"Stay still a second, Galena. I'm going to cut

one of your curls to show you."

Before she could protest, I snipped a curl from the back of her head and held it out to her.

There was a gasp from her translator box. I guess they don't cut hair on Ylepithon.

"Is that from me?" She took the curl and held it in her hand, turning it over and over, examining it closely. "How wonderful! Let's cut more," her voice tinkled.

"Oh, no you don't. I don't want your father on my case. For all I know, maybe it doesn't grow back where you come from."

"But I like it! Please, Lisa."

"Nope!" I said firmly as she reached for the scissors. Sometimes Galena acted very mature, but other times she behaved like the little kid she really was.

Dinner would be ready any moment. Galena seemed so fascinated with the scissors, and the idea of cutting more hair, that I thought if I took them with me, she might just follow me. But I couldn't leave them anywhere within her reach. I looked around the room.

"Li . . . sa, dinner's ready," Mom's voice floated up our trusty air register.

"Coming," I shouted back.

I spied a hook in the ceiling where I'd had a hanging ivy last year. Naturally, the ivy had died because I'd forgotten to water it. I dragged the chair from my desk under it and by balancing on tiptoe, I could just catch the handle of the scissors over the hook.

Galena showed no interest in my manoeuvers. Maybe she wouldn't touch the scissors, but I wasn't taking any chances. I dragged the chair back to the desk. Hearing a scratch at the door, I let Roper in. Mom must have dried him off and let him in the house. Sometimes he's scared of thunder and likes to hide in my room.

"I'm coming back later, Galena. Wait until you hear about the alpacas." She continued to look at me with seeming indifference.

"You and Roper can watch the storm until I get back." I stopped, my hand on the doorknob. "Do you have storms on Ylepithon?" I asked.

"No. but I was in a storm like this the other day with Christopher Columbus. It was exciting!"

No storms on Ylepithon. No cutting of hair. No friends, and no love. What a weird place it must be. No wonder Galena was so strange, I thought to myself as I ran downstairs for dinner.

CHAPTER 9

During dinner Mom commented that she was glad I'd washed the mousse out of my hair. She thought my hair didn't look so bad now, although she still preferred its natural color.

Smiling, Dr. Ferguson winked at me. I was surprised he hadn't told her what had happened. When I thought of how funny I must have looked, I began to chuckle.

"What's so funny?" Mom asked.

"Oh, nothing really." I cut the crust off my pie and pushed it to the rim of the plate where it wouldn't "infect" the rest of my pie. "I guess I'm just pleased that the alpacas are cute, puff ball animals rather than big birds. They're going to be fun to look after, especially the crias. The black one is my favorite. Can we call her 'Blacky'?"

Dr. Ferguson laughed. "Well, her proper registered name is 'Black Princess of Lace', but we can call her 'Blacky' for short."

"Ted says we're expecting two more crias

soon," Mom added. "Won't that be exciting?"

"Wow! For real?" I could hardly wait.

"For real!" Dr. Ferguson assured me. "Speaking of the alpacas, I'd better go back to check on them. Why don't you two wait until the rain lets up a little." He grabbed his slicker from the closet.

I helped Mom clear the table and load the dishwasher. Then I retrieved my school bag from the front hall where I'd dropped it when I'd first come home.

Suddenly Roper was whining at my side and scratching my leg with his paw. There was such a pleading in his eyes, I knew he wanted me to follow him. Something was the matter with Galena!

Dropping the bag, I raced Roper up the stairs. Through the open door my eyes first searched the ceiling. What a relief! The scissors were still on the hook. I'd had this terrible feeling that somehow Galena had managed to get a hold of those scissors.

When my gaze shifted to Galena on the bed, I nearly fainted! She was perched amid a pile of golden curls, laughing and playing with them.

"Oh no, Galena," I moaned.

"Look Lisa, my hair is cut too!" she announced proudly.

I looked up at the scissors and back at Galena. "How did you do that?" I demanded angrily. But she wouldn't tell me. Roper, who could only speak "dog", just whined uneasily and gave one little woof of apology.

"A simple 'sorry' won't do it, Roper. Galena's hair is a mess. What is Gagar going to say? Galena, at least I went to a hairdresser who cut it all the same length. You've chopped yours off all different lengths. It looks like a rat tried to eat your hair! We're going to have to even it out a bit."

Once again, I dragged the chair under the hook and retrieved the scissors. I was still utterly mystified about how she had got hold of them and put them back.

Galena was quite happy to sit very still and watch more golden curls fall onto her lap. I tried to even her hair out as much as possible without making it too short.

Gagar had explained that Galena was developing a unique power which would be important to Ylepithon's future. What if, like Samson's strength, the source of her power was in her hair, and here I was cutting it off? Maybe she was the only being on Ylepithon with hair! Maybe she was the future ruling princess of Ylepithon! I hoped Gagar would not be too mad at me.

Finally, I wet her hair with a spray bottle from the bathroom and blew it dry. Galena clearly enjoyed the whole procedure.

Instead of masses of long golden curls, she now had masses of short golden curls. She looked kind of cute . . . well, as cute as she could look, under the circumstances.

"You know, Galena, here on Earth, when kids feel neglected they sometimes act up and do weird things." The thought that this observation might well apply to my own actions of this afternoon nibbled at the edge of my consciousness, but I firmly ignored it. "I haven't been spending much time with you, because I didn't think you needed it, but now I think you do."

I gathered up all her curls and stuffed them in a little bag to send home with her. If it was important enough, maybe Ylepithon's technology could reattach them to her head.

I realized I hadn't even checked her nourishment band recently.

"There are an awful lot of green bumps left Galena." The look on her face told me she felt the same way about some vegetables as I do— they're quite yucky. However, Gagar insisted she had to eat them. I'd have to figure a way to accomplish that.

"You should see the alpacas, Galena. They're so cute. You'll love them. Won't she, Roper?" He thumped his tail enthusiastically on the floor, although I doubt that the word "alpaca" meant anything to him yet.

"I was going to sneak you down to the barn later tonight, but that rain doesn't look like quitting. Let's see your IDs. I'll bet there's something about alpacas."

I glanced at the cover of the IDs box where she always neatly filed the used ones. She hadn't gone through nearly as many as I'd expected, considering how much time she spent with them. I knew better than to ask her why. Galena knew enough to ignore a question that might get her in trouble.

"Is one of these an index that tells you where to find things?" I asked. She nodded as she solemnly picked out a disk and inserted it for a moment. Then she dumped the box of IDs on the bed and pawed through them until she found the right one.

She held the tiny gold disk up to me. "*The Ancient Mayan Civilization of South America.*" she said. "That's where alpacas lived in ancient times."

"Okay, you study that one, while I do my homework. We'll study together. Tomorrow I'll show you our alpacas. Roper, stay here, I'll be right back."

This time, I took the scissors with me—just to be absolutely sure!

CHAPTER 10

W hen I awoke next morning, the first birds were beginning to chirp, and the sun's rosy glow was creeping over the horizon. I quietly slipped out of bed, trying not to disturb Galena. She rolled over and a little hand crept over to my warm spot on the pillow.

"Sh. . . sh, Galena," I whispered as she opened her eyes groggily. I took her hand. "It's early. Go back to sleep." She slowly closed her eyes again. I waited until I was sure she was asleep to extract my hand from her tight little grip. I found Tedu and tucked him under her arm before pulling the sheet up to her chin.

Hopping off the bed without a sound, Roper followed me out the door, downstairs and outside. No one else would be up for at least a half an hour, but I was too excited to sleep any longer.

Cautioning Roper to stay quiet, I left him at the gate and ran to the barn to feed and water the alpacas as I'd promised Dr. Ferguson I would.

They were all kushed (that's what you call it when alpacas lie down and tuck their legs under them), but they quickly stood up and shook themselves when I entered. They weren't as nervous this morning. I was able to catch Blacky and hug her. Her wet little nose reached up to touch me on the cheek when I let her go. Then with a snort, she kicked up her hind legs to bound out of the barn, the white cria in pursuit. They zipped around the pasture, leaping in the air and bumping playfully into each other before returning to their mothers and breakfast.

After I doled out hay in the feeders, I watched the alpacas eat. They buried their heads in the hay to get the fine stuff at the very bottom of the feeder. When they brought their heads back up, their faces were barely visible through all the hay stuck on their heads. When they hummed and squealed to one another over breakfast, their heads held high, most of the hay fell onto the crias backs, so that soon they resembled miniature walking haystacks!

Finally, I checked my watch and left, realizing I'd be late for school if I didn't hurry. Scanning the sky for clouds on my way back to the house, I decided there was no threat of rain. I could risk wearing mousse today.

Paul was not impressed when I plunked myself down beside him on the bus.

"Oh no," he moaned. "I should have known you'd do something crazy like this. Are you nuts? Do you think Michael's going to like you better now?"

I sniffed. "I don't want Michael to like me! I did this to show him what red hair really looks like, since he doesn't seem to know."

"Well, you certainly are showing him. Did you have to cut it and spike it as well? Girls that do that are weirdos!" He stared morosely out the window for the rest of the trip. He didn't even ask about Galena!

I didn't think I looked that bad. The bright red had made my face look quite pale so I'd borrowed a bit of green eye shadow, mascara, and lipstick from Mom's drawer and put it on after I left the house. Paul was just going to have to learn to appreciate my creative side, I thought, as the bus arrived at school.

I soon discovered that most of the kids, like Paul, thought I was weird. As I walked down the hall to the classroom, groups of kids would turn away and become quiet as I approached. As soon as I passed, they started whispering.

Diane and Jenny, the two girls I kind of counted as friends, approached me in the cloakroom as I was hanging up my bag.

"What did you do that for?" Diane asked, wrinkling her nose up as she gave me the once over.

" 'Cause I wanted to, that's why!" I retorted hotly.

"You look weird, Lisa," she said with her nose still wrinkled up.

Jenny rolled her eyes. "I think you look gross." She walked away before I could even reply, which is probably just as well.

I hadn't anticipated these reactions. I had been so mad at Michael that I'd done this solely for the effect it would have on him. Now I was being ostracized by everyone. It wasn't a nice feeling.

And Michael? Michael didn't seem to care. He didn't tell me I looked weird, and he didn't tell me that now he could see the difference between red hair and auburn hair. He didn't say anything. He just looked at me a couple of times with an amused look, and then went about his own business.

This was not at all what I'd expected! I was even more annoyed when the principal, Ms. Watkins, stopped me in the hall and asked me to step into her office.

"Lisa, I understand your appearance is distracting some of the people in your class," she began, peering at me sternly above her granny glasses. I assumed "people" meant Mr. Thomas, although he hadn't actually said anything. He'd just grimaced when I walked in the door.

"Since we can't tolerate such distractions in a learning environment, I'm asking you to wash the make-up off now and come with a more appropriate hair style tomorrow."

I had to bite my tongue to keep from saying that I was just expressing my individuality, and that if the case were taken to the Supreme Court of Canada, I would probably win. It was against the Constitution to tell people how they could wear their hair, wasn't it?

"Yes, Ms. Watkins," I replied instead. I turned to leave.

"Lisa . . ."

I halted at the door.

"Mrs. Smith, our counsellor, would be happy to talk with you if you have a problem."

I gritted my teeth.

"I don't have a problem, and I don't want to see the counsellor. May I go now?" Why didn't anyone see that it was Michael who had the problem, not I.

"Yes, you may go."

The tone of her voice told me she thought she'd lost the opportunity to "save" one more doomed grade sixer.

Embarrassed, I snuck from her office to the washroom without anyone seeing me. The soap from the dispensers did not work well on mascara and lipstick. When I finished drying my face with paper towels, my eyes were surrounded with dark smudges. This gave me a haunted, forlorn look—which suited my mood perfectly.

At lunchtime, I wandered aimlessly around the school yard, feeling sorry for myself. Track and field season was starting and the tryouts for triple jump were today. I soon found myself standing next to Brad Summers at the triple jump pit.

It suddenly occurred to me that I was feeling the way Brad Summers probably felt most of the time—rejected by his classmates. The difference was that he usually did something to bug people, while I certainly hadn't done anything to bug anyone. But I still didn't like that feeling!

We watched in silence as one after another of the kids ran down the path, trying to make sure they took off from behind the white line for the hop, step and jump into the pit.

It looked like fun. I hadn't thought I knew the steps well enough to try out for it this year, but now it didn't look so hard. Maybe next year I'd go out for the track and field team.

Michael was next in line. He was a good all round athlete who would definitely make the track and field team and very likely win a first prize at the zonal competition. He was wonderful to watch. Sometimes he arced so high, he nearly cleared the pit. Everyone cheered him on.

Today, I didn't want Michael to think I was one of his admirers. As he started his run down the path, I turned to Brad.

"So, how's your assignment coming?" I asked.

Brad turned around to see who I was talking to. I guess he couldn't believe someone was initiating a conversation with him.

"Brad, I'm talking to you." I said.

"You are?" he asked, dumbfounded.

Out of the corner of my eye, I saw Michael trip on his shoelace and take off in a cartwheel across the pit. A collective sigh of sympathy rose from the onlookers. I turned away.

"Yes, I am. How's your Friendship Booklet coming?"

Brad blushed and kicked at a clump of grass.

"I haven't started it yet."

"Oh, yeah? How come?" I asked.

" 'Cause I can't do it."

"Maybe I could help you." The words tumbled out of me unexpectedly. When I realized what I'd said, I could hardly believe it. I'm not sure if

I was hoping to make Michael jealous, or if I was just feeling a bit empathetic towards Brad because of how I'd been treated that day. Whatever the reason, it was too late to retract my offer.

Brad's face went even redder. "You'd help me?"

I shrugged. "Well, you know, I could give you some ideas or something—if you want," I added quickly, hoping that maybe he'd reject any help.

"Yeah, I do need ideas, that's for sure." He finally looked at me. "You're certain you want to help me?"

"I offered, didn't I?" We both started walking back to the school. I swallowed hard. It was too late to withdraw now. "Why don't you come to my place after school tomorrow? I haven't started my project either. We can work together."

He gave me a long look, I guess to make sure I wasn't kidding.

"Okay . . . thanks." He bent his head down, and walked away rapidly.

"Lisa," Paul called, running up beside me as the bell rang. "I guess I was kind of mean this morning. You do crazy things sometimes, but I don't really think you're a weirdo." We walked towards the school together.

"I like you better without make-up," he blurted out suddenly.

"Well, you'll be happy to know that the spikes have to go by tomorrow also," I responded.

"Yeah, we heard."

Great! The whole school probably knew what had happened in Ms. Watkin's office.

"Hey," Paul said, "Cheer up, will you. It's not the end of the world. Can I come over after school to see Galena?"

I grabbed Paul's arm. "I forgot until now. You have to come over. You just have to. The alpacas came last night. They're soooo cute!"

"Really? Wow, I can hardly wait!"

The afternoon dragged on forever. Out of boredom I finally made a trip to the washroom. As I looked in the mirror, I had to admit that I did look rather goofy. A lot of unpleasant incidents had happened today. I hoped that the offer to help Brad Summers would not turn out to be the most unpleasant of all.

CHAPTER 11

When I got home from school, a note on the kitchen table informed me that Mom had a doctor's appointment and would be home with Ted by five o'clock. That was strange. Mom hadn't mentioned being sick, although she had been pretty tired lately. Maybe she needed a vitamin shot or something.

I ran upstairs to check on Galena. She was sitting in her usual spot on the bed, clutching Tedu, while immersed in an ID. I glanced at the lid of the box again. She couldn't have studied much today since there weren't any more IDs stored there than yesterday.

I pushed the stop button on her translator box. Blinking, she smiled at me.

"Hi, Lisa." She looked drowsy, but happy.

"Hi Galena. What were you immersed in?"

She opened up the little compartment and handed me the disk.

"*The Best of Children's Literature*," I read. "I bet that's fascinating!"

She nodded.

"Li...sa," Paul's voice called from the outside.

"Coming," I hollered back. "Come on Galena, I want to show you the alpacas."

A look of fright crossed her face as she shrank back.

"It's okay. Mom and Dr. Ferguson aren't here. It's just Paul and Roper down there."

She stared at me, still unconvinced.

"Do you realize you haven't been out of this room since you came? Who knows how long it will be before Gagar comes back for you." I put my arms out to her. "Come on. I promise nothing will hurt you. Bring Tedu if you want. I'll even carry you."

Reluctantly, she allowed me to pick her up, clutching Tedu.

"Here we go," I sang out as we went downstairs. "Galena, please don't hang on so tightly. You're using your stranglehold on me again."

On the way out, I grabbed a couple of carrots from the fridge. All of a sudden, I heard a loud hiss. I turned to see a terrified Tiffy plastered against the chair, her green eyes frozen on Galena. Her ears were flat against her head, her tail was fluffed to twice its normal size.

Yowling, she leapt off the chair and streaked

for the door. At that moment, Paul opened the door to check on where I was. Roper stuck his head in just as Tiffy bolted past. It was so good to see Tiffy afraid of something that I started to laugh.

Galena laughed too. "What was that?" she demanded.

"That was a cat, Galena," Paul said. "A scaredy cat!" He laughed at his own joke.

"She didn't tolerate me, did she?" Galena asked.

I smiled. "No, I don't think she even liked you. But never mind. She won't hurt you."

Galena clung tightly to Tedu and me while Paul ran ahead to the barn. I tried to imagine what it would be like if I'd never seen this world before: the carpet of green grass, the lazy white clouds drifting through the sapphire sky, dark scented evergreens, and birds singing in the trees. Galena knew from her IDs what everything was, but could she really appreciate the world through IDs alone?

"Wow, I see what you mean. They *are* cute," Paul exclaimed as we entered the barn.

Galena's grip suddenly relaxed and Tedu dropped unnoticed to the ground.

"Oh...h...h," she sighed.

The crias stepped forward, humming softly, followed by the moms. They showed no fear, no hesitant curiosity. They approached as if their single purpose was to greet Galena. As their large black eyes met Galena's large black eyes, I sensed an intimate communication flow between them, as if they were old friends meeting again. Perhaps, in some strange way, they recognized each other from ancient times. I hugged each cria, burying my face in their sweet smelling fluffy necks.

This happy mood was shattered when Paul heard a car door slam and announced that my mom and Dr. Ferguson were back.

They were early! What were we going to do with Galena? They would come to the barn as soon as they found the house empty. There was no time to hide Galena.

"Lisa, are you down here?" Mom's voice called from the gate.

"Not a word Galena." I warned her. "Just hang on to me and keep absolutely still."

"Hi, Paul. I didn't know you were here." Mom and Dr. Ferguson stepped through the doorway. They both stopped short, staring at Galena.

"In Heaven's name, what is that?" Mom burst out.

"It's a doll. Well, sort of. She's our mascot. Paul and I found her at a flea market. Isn't she cute?" I babbled.

"Well, I'd hardly go that far." Mom hesitated, still eyeing Galena. "She's very strange looking." She glanced at Dr. Ferguson and coughed slightly. "What's her name?"

I looked at Paul. "Actually, her name is Galena and she's from the planet Ylepithon."

Dr. Ferguson nodded his head, laughing. "Galena from the planet Ylepithon, eh? I swear, Lisa, someday your creative imagination will make you very rich!"

I laughed a little too. "Look, we've got to go. Paul's late for something. Aren't you, Paul?"

"Oh yeah, I am. I'm late. Bye, Auntie Kay. Bye Dr. Ferguson."

"Just a minute, Paul. You may as well hear the news too, since you're family." A smile lit up Mom's face.

"Lisa, you're going to have a little brother or sister in five months. Paul, you'll have another cousin. Ted and I are having a baby."

Paul glanced quickly at me, uncertain how I was going to react.

"That's great, Auntie Kay." He stopped and, seeing me speechless, continued. "I really have to go now. Can I tell Mom though?"

Mom hadn't stopped smiling since her announcement. "I'll go and phone her in a few minutes. Let me tell her, okay?"

"Okay. Bye, Lisa, I'll call you later."

Paul may be growing up, but he's still a chicken when it comes to sticking around when there's trouble. He disappeared up the path.

"But you're too old," I wailed.

"No, I'm not. The doctor says I'm fine."

"But we don't need another person in our family," I wailed again.

I think Mom finally realized that I wasn't quite as happy about all this as she was. Her smile gave way to a look of concern.

"Oh, Lisa." She stepped forward to hug me. I knew I couldn't stand a hug right now.

Brushing between her and Dr. Ferguson, I gripped Galena tightly and fled to the house and into my room. I locked the door, although I was sure that Dr. Ferguson would suggest Mom leave me alone for awhile.

Then I cried myself to sleep while Galena sat beside me, stroking my hair.

CHAPTER 12

By the time Brad came over after school the next day I had spread a bunch of old magazines on the dining room table. If we started with something simple like the poster, I was hoping he could do the rest himself.

He arrived with a scowl on his face. "This is a dumb assignment," he muttered as he walked in.

I frowned at him. "It's going to be fun—at least it *was* going to be fun," I said pointedly.

Brad ignored me as he leafed through a magazine.

"Bet you're sorry you said you'd help me," he retorted without looking up.

"I'm beginning to be," I said hotly. I shoved a magazine into his hand. The picture on the cover showed two kids tobogganing. "There's your first picture. Cut it out."

Still scowling, he started cutting. I found a picture of a girl with her horse. That's the kind of friendship I'd like to have, I thought, cutting it out.

Brad cut the picture out very carefully. For some reason I'd expected him to be careless and sloppy.

"How come you haven't any friends?" I asked, without stopping to think.

Brad turned all red. "I've got lots of friends," he said.

"You do not!"

"How do you know?"

"Well, I see you every day at school. You don't seem to get along with anyone very well," I replied.

"Maybe all my friends are outside of school," Brad muttered.

"No, they're not. I overheard you tell Mr. Thomas you'd never had a friend."

Brad didn't look up. He didn't say anything—he just kept cutting. Then he picked up another magazine and started on another picture. Halfway through cutting it out, he put down the scissors. He gazed past me, out the window.

"Once, I had sort of a friend—a younger brother—but he died." He sighed. "That's when we started moving. We moved four times before we came here."

We continued in silence for a while, lost in our own thoughts.

Roper scratched at the door. I let him in and

continued into the kitchen for milk and cookies.

To my surprise, when I came back, Roper was talking to Brad. That's unusual for Roper. He usually hangs back a bit until he is used to a new person. But there he was, a paw up on Brad's leg, wagging his tail, while he pushed his wet nose against Brad's hand.

"Looks like you've just made a friend," I said, handing Brad a cookie. He promptly broke it in two and gave Roper half.

"Now you've got a friend for life," I laughed.

A small smile tugged at Brad's mouth. He stroked Roper's silky ears.

"Sure wish I could have a dog," he said in a low voice.

"Why can't you?" I asked.

" 'Cause the house we rent won't take animals." He sighed. "Besides, Mom says we couldn't afford a dog."

"It can't be that expensive to keep a dog," I argued.

Brad's face turned a bit red. "Everything's too expensive when your Dad's left and your Mom works for minimum wage."

I stopped cutting, remembering what our lives had been like before Dr. Ferguson and my mom were married.

"Yeah, that's true," I said.

Roper lay down against Brad's feet and fell asleep. We resumed snipping out pictures. Soon we had a pile of clippings showing many different interpretations of friendship. I wasn't sure Mr. Thomas would accept the one of a girl sitting under a tree with a book, but I was ready to argue that I have many books that are friends, as well as a few trees that are special friends.

I found the poster paper I'd brought from school. Once again, Brad was very careful. He spread out his pictures, re-arranging them several times before he was satisfied enough to glue them on.

I checked my watch. "We'll have to stop in a few minutes. I've got to start chores."

Brad carefully glued his last picture and rolled the poster up. I handed him an elastic.

"Did you get some ideas so that you can do the rest on your own?" I asked.

"Yeah, I guess so," Brad replied as he stood up. Startled out of his doggy dreams, Roper leapt to his feet. Brad watched as I stacked the magazines and cleaned the scraps off the table. He shifted uneasily from one foot to the other.

"Could I... could I come over tomorrow and take Roper for a walk?" He spoke hesitantly with a pleading look in his eyes.

"Sure," I answered quickly. He turned to leave.

"I'll be writing my poem tomorrow. If you want to, after you take Roper for a walk, we could work on our poems together."

A smile spread across Brad's face. I swear it was the first time I'd ever seen him really truly smile.

"Yeah, okay." He patted Roper's head. "Thanks. See ya."

I ran upstairs to change out of my school clothes. Roper loped along behind me to the top of the stairs. Then he pushed past me, tail wagging, to greet Galena.

CHAPTER 13

Galena was asleep on the bed. Asleep! Galena never slept in the day time. She led her life in such an orderly fashion; pushing buttons to eat, immersing herself all day in IDs to learn, and sleeping all night—but never in the day.

My heart skipped a beat. Maybe she was sick. Tiptoeing over to her, I felt her forehead to see if she was hot before realizing how silly that was. Who said Ylepithons get hot like humans do when they're sick?

Opening her translator box, I ejected the ID. It was *The Best of Children's Literature*, the same one she'd used yesterday. Glancing at the IDs she'd finished, I realized the number hadn't increased for some time. A sneaking suspicion crept into my mind.

"Galena, wake up." I tugged at her arm. Slowly she opened her eyes, smiled and sat up.

"Lisa. I was having such a wonderful dream. Eyore and I were walking through the woods and . . . "

"Eyore? Eyore from *Winnie the Pooh*?"

Her eyes grew wide. "You know *Winnie the Pooh*?"

"Of course I know *Winnie the Pooh*! Everyone knows *Winnie the Pooh*! It's a classic!"

I held up the ID. "Galena, how many times have you immersed yourself in this?"

She wouldn't look at me. Nor would she answer.

"You've been using this one over and over for some time, haven't you? Gagar told me to make sure you went through them all. You're ignoring your education about Earth."

"I don't care!" Galena said petulantly. "Who wants to learn about all that stuff when they can be a part of wonderful stories like *Winnie the Pooh* or *Charlotte's Web* or *Wrinkle in Time*?"

Even though I couldn't admit it, I could certainly agree with that. Mom had been buying me books since I was a baby. I'd added all my favorites as I grew older. By now, I had quite a collection. I pulled one from the bookcase.

"Look, Galena, I have *Charlotte's Web* too."

She clapped her hands in delight. "Let me see it, please."

She took it from my hands and turned it over and over without opening the cover. Finally she looked up at me. "This is a very unusual ID. Where can I plug in my translator wire?"

I laughed. "No, Galena, this is a book." Taking it from her, I sat on the bed and opened it. "Look, you have to read the words. Can you read?"

"Yes, I can read. I learned about it from the ID on the history of the printing press." She pointed to a word. "Each of those symbols makes a sound. When you put them together they make words, and many words make a story. But that's so slow and boring."

"No, it's not. Here on Earth, moms and dads often read stories to their kids, especially at bedtime. When kids hear the stories they make pictures in their minds—that's the fun part! It puts them to sleep, just like your ID did. When I was younger, my favorite part of the day was having Mom read to me."

Gazing out of the window, I remembered how good it had felt. My insides twisted. Those days were long gone. Soon Mom would be reading to someone else.

"Show me how it's done, Lisa. Read *Charlotte's Web* to me, please," Galena pleaded, breaking into my thoughts.

Galena had been gaining all her knowledge about our planet through IDs. It was time she learned about life on Earth by experiencing it.

"Okay. Well, usually the mom or dad sits close to the child, like this. It just feels better that way." I propped a pillow up next to Galena and snuggled down. Patting the bed for Roper, who was begging to come up, I began reading.

"This is a good story because it's about a farm. I wish Wilbur was an alpaca, though, instead of a pig," Galena interrupted.

"Yes. Shhh now. You don't talk during a story. You just listen."

Galena leaned her head against my shoulder. "Okay."

She didn't say another word. When I turned the page she took my arm and put it around her, which made turning pages a bit awkward. I needn't have worried. By the time I was ready to turn the next page, Galena had crept up onto my lap and pulled my arms snugly around her tummy. As I read, she turned the pages.

It had been such a long time since I'd read *Charlotte's Web*, that I found myself enjoying it as much as I ever had. I don't know how many chapters I finished before all three of us fell asleep.

I woke up suddenly when Mom tapped on the door.

"Lisa, you forgot your chores again!" She sighed. "You've been better at remembering lately, but we have to be able to count on you."

I rubbed my eyes. "I didn't really forget,

Mom. I came up here to change my clothes and..." I looked down at Galena, who had frozen into "doll" mode at Mom's appearance, "...and...well...I guess I did forget. I'll go do them right now."

"No, never mind. Ted's done them. It's almost dinner time." Looking down at Galena, she frowned. "This was down at the barn." She set Tedu on the dresser. "You're quite attached to that funny looking doll, aren't you? It's strange. You never were one to play with dolls."

She sat down on the edge of the bed. I quickly lifted Galena off my lap and propped her in the corner where she stayed, motionless. I swung my feet around to sit beside Mom.

"You're okay, aren't you? I mean, I could get Dr. Melville to recommend a counsellor if you'd like to talk to someone."

I clenched my teeth. "Why does everyone think I need a counsellor? I'm fine. And I don't need a counsellor!"

Suddenly Mom put her arms around me, pulling me close. "Lisa, I realize I haven't been a very good Mom to you lately. I've been so busy getting used to marriage with Ted, that I've kind of taken you for granted. I should have realized you might not be as keen about this baby as I am, but you don't need to worry." Still holding me, she looked into my eyes. "I'll never love you any less."

My feelings became all jumbled up. Mom didn't usually say things like that. For a moment I wanted to cry.

"You know what?" she said. "I think we need to spend some time together each week—just the two of us. How would you like that?"

"That would be good," I ventured. "What kind of things?" I hoped she wouldn't suggest bowling or something equally boring.

"Well, you appear to have grown in the last few months. You probably could do with some new clothes. Why don't you and I go out for dinner this Friday night and go shopping afterwards? Next week, you think of something."

"Cool," I answered, smiling.

Mom picked up *Charlotte's Web*. "Remember when I used to read to you every night? Wasn't that fun? Maybe this time, we can take turns reading to your little brother or sister."

I considered this for a moment. "Yeah, that might be okay."

Out of the corner of my eye, I suddenly saw Tedu rise in the air and do a little wiggle before plopping back softly onto the dresser. Roper whined.

Mom set the book down, stroked Roper on the

head, and stood up. "I'm sure by now Ted's started dinner. I'd better go see." She bent over and kissed me on the cheek. "We're going to have lots of fun with the baby—all of us."

I smiled. "I'll be down in a minute."

As soon as she left, I turned to Galena. She was staring at Tedu, concentrating fiercely. Tedu's foot wiggled. He danced into the air again before falling back to the dresser. A second later, he rose gracefully into the air to sail over my head into her outstretched arms.

"Wow!" I gasped. "Did you do that, Galena?"

She nodded.

"That's the unique power Gagar told me about. You're learning to move things with your mind by concentrating on them. You're practising levitation, aren't you?" I thought for a moment. "The scissors! That's how you got the scissors to cut your hair."

Galena smiled.

"You had a lot of nerve to move something in front of Mom. You're lucky she didn't see it."

"She was talking too long," Galena said, hugging Tedu. It seemed as if Galena didn't want to share me, in the same way I didn't want to share Mom.

"I think you've just acquired another emotion," I told her. "It's called jealousy!"

Ignoring my comment, Galena picked up *Charlotte's Web*. "Please read some more."

"No, I've got to go for dinner." I pulled back her sleeve to look at her wristband. "I'll make a deal with you. You eat some vegetables every day and start going through different IDs, like you're supposed to, and I'll read to you every night."

"Like we did tonight, with me on your lap, and Roper there too?"

"Yes, just like that," I promised.

She held up her hands, fingers apart. "It's a deal. Will you read to me tonight?"

I turned at the door. "What are you having for dinner?"

"Four green bumps!" Galena promised.

I smiled. "I'll be back in a couple of hours."

CHAPTER 14

The days had quickly turned into weeks and we still hadn't heard anything from Gagar. I hoped nothing had gone wrong. Galena kept her promise to eat her vegetables and immerse herself in different IDs, and I kept mine about reading to her every night. We finished *Charlotte's Web* and started *Anne of Green Gables*, which Galena found fascinating. Roper enjoyed this nightly ritual too. He made sure that he never missed story time. Sometimes a glazed look came over his eyes as I read, and I wondered what kind of pictures were forming in his doggy head.

Something else Galena and I did every night was to slip down to visit the alpacas. We chose a time when Mom and Dr. Ferguson were busy with something else, so Galena could really play with them.

I'd ended up working with Brad through most of the Friendship assignment. I hadn't planned it that way. It's just that he kept asking to take

Roper for walks. Since Roper enjoyed the walks, how could I say no? Usually when he arrived, I'd be working on some part of the assignment, and before long, we'd be working on it together.

Not that I minded. To my total surprise, Brad was turning into an okay person. He even smiled sometimes now. When he did, his face lit up and a dimple appeared, making him look kind of cute. There was a subtle change in the way kids at school were treating him, and the way he was treating them. No one called him "Worm Face" any more. Maybe finding a friend like Roper was all Brad needed.

"I don't think it's Roper, I think it's you that Brad likes," Paul said laughing.

It was Sunday, and he had come over to help me clean out the alpaca pens.

My shovel stopped in mid-air. "Me? Don't be goofy!"

Paul leaned on his shovel, looking at me. "I'm not being goofy. It's true! He told me he likes your hair that way. He had kind of a sappy look on his face when he said it. That's got to mean he likes you."

My hand reached up to sweep over my short hair. I could feel my face turn red. I quickly changed the subject.

"You haven't heard my great news!"

Mom and Dr. Ferguson had told me over breakfast. Ever since, I'd been carrying the words inside me like a ray of warm sunshine. I was almost afraid to say them out loud for fear they'd shatter and disappear.

"The next cria that's born is going to be mine!" There, the words were out. They danced and shimmered in the air, but they didn't disappear. It must be true! I hugged myself in delight.

"Wow, how come?" Paul dropped his shovel and followed me to the fence to look at the two alpacas who were expecting babies. Butterscotch was gold, with long, soft, silky fleece. Copper was a deep rust and very fluffy. I didn't care which one was going to have my cria. They were both beautiful!

"Well, it's kind of a business proposition they told me. It's a future payment for the work I do now. I'll have to sell it in a couple of years, and put the money away for university. If it's a female, then it can have babies too, and I'll have more money for university."

"When will it be born?" Paul asked eagerly.

I looked at the two females critically. Their thick fleece made them so round and fluffy, they didn't look any different from the others.

"Dr. Ferguson says that before alpacas were domesticated their ancestors had to be able to run fast to escape predators, so alpacas carry their babies high up under the ribs where they're out of the way. Even though the mothers don't look pregnant, he thinks both cria will be born within a week or two."

"You're so lucky," Paul muttered.

"You can help me with the cria any time you want," I said. "We'll have to get it used to our touch, and later, halter train it because I'll want to show it."

Paul smiled his approval. We went back to work and finished cleaning the pen. Later Dr. Ferguson would come with the tractor to move the pile on to the alfalfa field as fertilizer.

"I'm going to take Galena to school tomorrow," I said, as the thought occurred to me.

Paul gasped. "Are you nuts? You'll never get away with it."

"Sure I will. Remember, it's only half a day tomorrow because of parent-teacher interviews. I want her to experience more about what it's really like on Earth. Having her come to school will show her how we learn," I answered. "Besides, she's very good at acting like a doll. I can always sit her in my locker with an ID when she's had enough. She'll understand."

"She'll move something in her weird way and get us in trouble," Paul warned.

Galena seemed to be mastering her new power pretty quickly. Lately, she'd been using it to tease me. Last night, every time I went to fill a feed bucket, it would move out of my reach. When I tried to halter one of the moms to practise leading her around, the halter jumped out of my hand and stayed in mid-air just out of my reach. Meanwhile, Galena sat laughing on a bale of hay. I finally had to threaten her with not bringing her to the barn if she didn't stop. I was sure, however, that I could impress on her the importance of behaving at school.

"She will. She'll move something," Paul repeated when I hadn't answered.

"No, she won't," I insisted.

CHAPTER 15

I persuaded Mom to drive me to school by claiming I didn't want to damage my Friendship assignment poster. The real reason was that the school bus was too crowded and I wasn't sure how the kids would react to Galena. I wanted to make sure she would be safe.

I had explained where we were going, and that I would carry her in my gym bag with just her head sticking out so she could wiggle her hands and toes from time to time. I had made her promise that she would not move anything with her mind. I'd shown her how to cross her heart when a promise is for real, although I wasn't sure that would apply in her case because she probably didn't have a heart like ours.

"You're sure you want to take that doll to school, Lisa?" Mom asked, frowning, as we climbed into the car.

"Yup, I'm sure," I replied. "I have to, she's part of my language arts assignment."

This, in fact, was true. Last night, after I had

suggested taking Galena to school, Paul and I decided we needed a good reason for taking her. We built our oral presentation around her.

Paul met me outside the school just before the bell. With Galena in the gym bag between us, we marched into the school, ignoring a few strange looks as we entered the classroom.

Jenny and Diane approached us. "What's that?" Jenny asked, pointing at Galena.

"She's our mascot. We found her at the flea market," Paul replied quickly.

"Really? She's kind of cute!" Jenny cooed.

If I'd have said what Paul did, Jenny probably would have laughed and called me weird. But ever since Paul had shown interest in Diane, Jenny had tried to get his attention. I think she was a bit jealous.

"What's her name?" Diane asked.

"Her name is Galena. She's from the planet Ylepithon. At least, that's what the sign on her said when we bought her," I added quickly.

"Cool!" Diane grinned. "Were there any more of them? I'd like to get one too."

Smiling, I shook my head. The rest of the kids crowded around for a look. Thankfully, Diane and Jenny had set the mood. Everyone thought Galena was cute. I looked at Paul and breathed a sigh of relief.

The oral presentations took up the first part of the morning. Brad hadn't told me what he was doing, but I wasn't surprised when he spoke about a dog being man's best friend. On the way back to his desk, our eyes met and I gave him a little thumbs up sign. He'd done a good job.

Although Michael's presentation was as usual very good, my mind wandered, and I realized with a jolt that I no longer cared about him. That made me feel good.

Just before our presentation, I took Galena into the washroom on the pretense of getting her ready. Actually, I knew she'd need a stretch. Unzipping the gym bag, I helped her out.

She clapped her hands in delight. "Oh Lisa, this is fun! I'm glad you brought me to school. I like your friends."

"You just like them because they think you're cute," I teased. It suddenly occurred to me that Galena had used the word "like", rather than "tolerate". Maybe she was beginning to understand some of Earth's strange emotions.

Back in class, I sat her on my knee while Paul and I made our presentation. The gist of it was that a "friend" can be anything—it doesn't have to be a person—as long as the object does something for you, like bring you comfort, or keep you company. For some little kids, a favorite blanket or soother becomes their friend. For older people maybe their car or their TV becomes their friend. For Paul and me, it was our mascot, Galena.

I think Mr. Thomas was impressed with our unusual presentation. He even agreed to let us take our mascot into the science room for the next period, as long as she was in the gym bag on a shelf by the door. If I'd guessed what was going to happen in science that day, I'd have left Galena at home and probably played sick myself.

CHAPTER 16

We'll continue our study of the human body today in science. Last period, we examined diagrams of the human eye. This period, I'm going to demonstrate the dissection of a sheep's eye," Mr. Thomas explained as everyone got settled.

He dramatically reached down into his briefcase and pulled out a small plastic bag. All the kids who were eager to see gross stuff like this crowded forward. A few of us hung back.

I didn't mind watching Dr. Ferguson suture little wounds and give shots, but studying somebody's eyeball when it's out of their head was not my idea of fun. Lately, I'd been thinking that I might like to be a veterinarian when I grew up. Now, I wasn't so sure.

From the plastic bag, Mr. Thomas pulled out an object the size of a ping pong ball. He held it up in front of his face for us all to see. For a moment the big black eye stared at us as if it were one of his. I shuddered. It looked exactly like one of Copper's or Butterscotch's eyes. On the desk in front of him, glinting in the sunlight, lay a razor sharp scalpel.

Mr. Thomas pointed out the iris and retina. He explained the fatty tissue at the back, and how the eye was connected to the eye socket. Then he reached for the scalpel.

As his hand approached the handle, the scalpel slid along the desk, out of his reach. Frowning, Mr. Thomas reached for it again. The scalpel skittered over the side of the desk, but instead of falling like any metal object, it dipped and dove around like a feather riding an air current. Mr. Thomas just watched it in amazement as it came to rest on the floor far from the desk.

Jenny inadvertently saved the day for Galena and me. She had hung back, a weird look on her face, when Mr. Thomas had pulled the eye out of the bag. Now, without warning, she threw up! When everyone turned to look, I took the opportunity to clutch my stomach and moan, "May I be excused? I think I'm going to be sick too!"

Mr. Thomas nodded quickly. I grabbed the gym bag and ran out. Jenny, totally embarrassed, collapsed sobbing in her desk.

As we walked home, Paul told me laughing,

that Mr. Thomas never had cut the sheep's eye. He'd said maybe another day. He must have been freaked out by the "flying" scalpel. He swept it into a dustpan and dumped it into the trash can rather than try to pick it up again. The class had returned to home room for silent reading until the end of the period because the science room smelled of vomit.

"It's early," I said, checking my watch. "Let's take Galena down to the creek to show her the flowers and fish. Not that you should be rewarded for breaking your promise, Galena." I patted her hands, which were around my neck. "I'm glad you did though. That eye looked too much like an alpaca eye!"

We clambered down the trail to the creek, Paul ahead of me.

"I don't know how I'll ever be a veterinarian," I mumbled, half to myself.

Paul turned to look back at me. "What, because of the eye? Don't be goofy. You have to remember, doing all that stuff teaches you how an animal is put together. That's how you learn to help them."

"I guess you're right," I said. Maybe some day Dr. Ferguson would let me help him more, so I could learn that way.

For the next couple of hours we enjoyed the

sunshine and delighted Galena by introducing her to real birds, fish and wildflowers.

When we finally got home, we discovered that Mom and Dr. Ferguson had left for my parent-teacher interview at school. Quickly Paul and I grabbed a snack and headed down to the barn with Galena.

CHAPTER 17

Both Butterscotch and Copper were munching on grass in the pasture, seemingly without a care in the world. When they spotted Galena, they wandered over to nuzzle her. As we neared the barn, Galena's grip tightened.

"Something's wrong with Blacky," her translator box murmured.

Paul ran ahead. "Lisa, come quickly!" he hollered.

Blacky lay very still in the corner. Her mom stood beside her, humming and nudging Blacky every few seconds. As we approached, the little cria lifted her head and looked at us with bright, anxious eyes. She struggled to stand up, but her back legs wouldn't support her.

Quickly lifting Galena off, I knelt beside Blacky. Normally she would have scrambled to her feet and permitted me a quick hug before dashing off. Now, she just lay there panting, her eyes full of fear.

"Oh no," I cried. I looked at Paul for help. "What can be wrong?"

He just shrugged, shaking his head. I gently ran my hands down and around each leg, checking for a possible broken leg. A stab of fear shot through me. Could she have been bitten by a rattlesnake?

I wondered how long she'd been ill. Maybe she needed a drink. Scooping up water out of the water trough, I knelt beside her once more. She took a few sips, then wearily lowered her head back on the ground.

"Stay here with her. I'm going to phone the school to see if I can reach Dr. Ferguson," I said, running for the house.

He wasn't there. The secretary checked the interview schedule. The interview with my teachers had been over an hour ago. He and my mom must be running errands around town. There was no way of telling when they'd be home.

I couldn't bear the thought of Blacky dying. Quite apart from the money she cost, money that our family could ill afford to lose, I couldn't bear to lose her!

It was all my fault. I should have been home to check on them right after school. I just wasn't responsible enough to have a cria of my own. I was sure that's what Dr. Ferguson would say.

Perhaps he was right! Angrily, I brushed the tears out of my eyes and started back to the barn.

"Li...sa," Paul yelled urgently, his head around the corner of the barn. I broke into a run.

"Is she...did she?"

"No, it's not that. Galena has examined Blacky, inch by inch. She thinks she's found the problem. Look!"

I bent over to look at the spot on Blacky's rump, where Galena was parting the fleece. She pointed to a small black bump the size of a pea.

"It's a tick!" Paul said excitedly. "I know because I had one on me last year and I had to go to the doctor to get it removed."

I'd learned about the problems ticks can cause animals from Dr. Ferguson. Ticks are small beetle-like insects that live in the grass in our area in late spring. When they latch onto a person or animal they embed their head into the skin and engorge themselves as they feed off the blood. If they're not discovered, they can cause paralysis, which starts in the legs and moves upward until finally it paralyzes the lungs, causing death.

I also knew that if the tick were removed in time, there was a good chance of total recovery. Peering at the bump, I realized that the tick's head was completely dug in to the skin. If I pulled on the body and left the head stuck, it would be even more difficult to remove.

I had no idea how quickly the paralysis progressed. Oh, why didn't Mom and Dr. Ferguson come home?

"I'm going to look for something to pull it out with," I decided finally.

"Wait a minute," Paul said pointing to Galena. She was kneeling by Blacky with that look of fierce concentration she wore when she was trying to move things with her mind. She stared determinedly at the tick.

Slowly, slowly, the tick backed out, head and all. The next thing we knew, it was lying belly up in her little hand. I guessed what would happen next.

"Don't squash it, Galena. We better keep it to show Dr. Ferguson. Hang on to it for a minute." I ran up to the clinic, returning with a bottle of antiseptic, a pair of tweezers, and a small jar.

With the tweezers, I gingerly lifted the horrid little insect from Galena's hand, plopped it in the bottle, and screwed the lid on tightly. Then I doused the tiny wound in Blacky's flank with antiseptic. It would be a while before we knew if Blacky would recover, but we'd now done everything we could think of.

When Galena hugged Blacky, the little cria

seemed to relax. Stretching her neck out on the ground, she watched us, her eyes less fearful.

Then I hugged Galena tightly. "For once, I'm glad you have that strange power, Galena! You may have saved Blacky's life!"

"Maybe Galena is developing into some sort of healer for Ylepithon and was sent to Earth to practise," Paul mused. "You should have seen the way she went over Blacky. It was almost as if she knew what she was looking for."

"Is that true, Galena?" I asked. "Gagar said you were meant for great things in the future of Ylepithon. Are you learning to be a healer, or a ruler?"

But Galena wouldn't answer. Maybe she didn't even know herself. She hugged Blacky again. The lights on her belt raced in circles, and I knew she was telling Blacky something we'd never know.

All three of us settled down to wait, watching Blacky closely for any changes. No one was willing to leave until we could tell whether she was going to get better or not. Finally, when Roper barked, we knew Mom and Dr. Ferguson had returned.

As I ran to the barn door to call them, Galena propped herself on a bale of hay in the corner.

I met them halfway to the barn. The relief at seeing them was so immense that I felt tears in my eyes again. I struggled to keep from crying and throwing myself in their arms as I wanted to.

"It's Blacky, Dr. Ferguson." I gulped before I could go on. "She was bitten by a tick and can't get up. I'm so glad you're home. We got the tick out, but we don't know what else to do!"

"Oh no!" Mom cried. Dr. Ferguson turned without a word and ran to the clinic for his veterinary bag.

Mom put her arms around both Paul and me as we watched Dr. Ferguson examine Blacky. I couldn't stop shaking. Suddenly, the tears that had threatened before, overflowed.

"It's all my fault. We went down to the creek instead of coming home right after school. This would never have happened if I'd have come straight home. I'm sorry, Mom. I'm sorry, Dr. Ferguson," I wailed.

His examination over, Dr. Ferguson rubbed Blacky affectionately on the head.

"That's not true, Lisa. You normally wouldn't have been home until now anyway. That tick has been on Blacky for at least a week in order to cause paralysis. Finding it a couple of hours earlier wouldn't have made much difference." He held up the jar to have a close look at the tick. "You did a very good job of removing the tick. They're very hard to pull out. How did you do it?"

I glanced at Paul, then at Galena. "Well, we just concentrated on getting it out in one piece, and it came."

"You handled things very responsibly. I'm proud of you." He smiled. "And Lisa, will you please, please, please stop calling me Dr. Ferguson. I think I've been a member of this family long enough for you to start calling me by some other name. I don't expect you to call me Dad, of course, although you'd be welcome to if you want to. But at least, try to call me Ted, okay?"

He looked at Blacky again. "All we can do now is wait. Let's leave her alone to rest while we have dinner."

"Paul," Mom said, "you're welcome to stay but you better phone your mom. I imagine you'd like to see if there's any change in Blacky after dinner."

I followed Mom out, leaving Galena behind on purpose. I knew she'd want to stay with Blacky.

"Lisa, Ted is proud of you because of the way you handled the problem with Blacky just now. And I'm proud of you because your teachers say you've been working really hard this term," Mom commented as we walked back to the house.

I smiled. If only Blacky recovered, the world would just about be perfect!

CHAPTER 18

The message from Gagar was crystal clear. It cut through the night and hung in the air, jolting me awake. His ship was full of super fleas and would not be landing on Earth. A sister ship on the mission would stop by for Galena. She was to wait on the back lawn at precisely 2:37 a.m. tomorrow morning to be picked up. Well, at least I wouldn't have to explain the matter of Galena's cropped hair to Gagar, I thought. She'd have to deal with that herself when she got home.

Roper whined beside me. I hushed him by stroking one of his silky ears. He had been restless all night because of Galena's absence. Now, maybe he too had received the message.

After dinner, there had been no change in Blacky. Paul had finally gone home. The rest of us had stayed at the barn until we were all exhausted. Dr. Ferguson—I mean Ted—finally said that we'd know one way or the other by morning, and we might as well go to bed. There was nothing more we could do but let nature take its course.

Checking my clock and finding it was 2:39 a.m. I quietly slipped out of bed. I shushed Roper as we snuck downstairs and out the door. Moonlight flooded the yard, creating ghostly shadows which raced along side of us down to the barn. Leaving Roper at the door, I stepped inside to switch on the light.

"Oh Lisa, you scared me!" Galena was standing beside Blacky who was up on wobbly legs, nursing.

"She's going to live!" I breathed a huge sigh of relief.

I quickly checked her over. She was still weak, but she could use her hind legs again. By morning, she'd probably be leaping in the air as she raced around the pasture. I gave Blacky a hug and turned to Galena, who watched me with a sad look in her eyes.

"You got your father's message, too, didn't you?" I asked as I picked her up. She threw her arms tightly around my neck.

"I don't want to go back, Lisa," she whimpered, burying her face in my neck.

"I don't want you to go back, either, Galena, but it's just not possible for you to stay here on Earth. You're needed on Ylepithon. You must go back."

Neither one of us spoke as I carried her back up to the house and tucked her into bed with Roper and me. I think it was a long time before any of us slept.

When I awoke, groggy and tired, I realized I'd slept later than usual. That wasn't a problem because it was Saturday. But I sensed that there was a problem: something wasn't right. I sat up to look around. I was alone! Where were Roper and Galena? I scrambled out of bed. Tedu and Galena's suitcase were missing too. Where could they all be?

Galena knew better than to wander around in broad daylight. She must have left soon after I'd gone to sleep. And Roper had gone with her.

Maybe they were down at the barn. I threw on my clothes and raced downstairs. No one was there. Beside my bowl and the cereal box on the table was a note telling me that Blacky was going to be okay. I smiled. I already knew that! Mom must be helping Dr. Ferguson—Ted—out at the clinic.

Ignoring breakfast, I ran down to the barn. It was empty. Even Blacky, looking completely recovered, was in the pasture with the rest of the alpacas. I plopped down on a bale of hay to think. Galena didn't want to return to Ylepithon. Now she'd run away. I should have guessed she might try a stunt like this. Thank goodness Roper was with her to keep her safe, but I needed help in finding her.

I ran back to the house and phoned Paul, explaining the message from Gagar and Galena's absence. Ten minutes later he pedalled up the driveway and skidded to a halt beside me.

He took one look at my face. "You still haven't found them! Where have you looked?" In the time it had taken Paul to ride over, I'd done a thorough search of the barn and house. If they were hiding there, Roper would have come out. I was sure he sensed that Galena shouldn't be taking off and had tagged along to look after her.

I began to panic.

"Okay, okay. Let's just calm down and think about this," Paul said, plunking himself down on the grass and breaking off a long piece to chew on. "Galena is too smart to run away in hopes of not being sent back to Ylepithon. She knows she can't be seen moving around on her own." He plucked another piece of grass. "Galena may have learned a lot, and maybe she'll be very important some day, but right now, I swear, she's just a bratty little kid."

With a snap of his fingers, he jumped up. "I bet I know where she's gone!"

"Where?"

"To the creek. Galena loved it there. Remember how fascinated she was by the fish and the butterflies?"

Paul was probably right.

We could reach the creek in five minutes by bicycle or fifteen by walking. The trail down to the creek was quite steep and overgrown. Riding our bikes back up would be tough going. We decided to walk, but before long, we were running, bending our heads to avoid branches, mindless of the tall grass which tried to ensnare our legs. At the bottom of the ravine, we stopped to catch our breath and then walked in the direction we'd gone with Galena before.

The babbling of the creek allowed us to spot her before she heard us. She sat on a rock by the edge of the creek, leaning against a tree. Her arms clasped around Tedu, the way she always pulled my arms around her, she was reading *Winnie the Pooh* to Tedu while Roper lay by the rock, his head on his paws.

I was so happy to see her safe and sound that I didn't know whether to hug or scold her.

She looked up as we approached. "Lisa, I'm reading to Tedu and Roper the way you taught me." Roper looked at me guiltily, thumping his tail on the ground.

I scratched his ear to tell him he was forgiven. "Galena, you shouldn't have wandered off like that. Paul and I were worried!"

"I didn't wander off. I was running away. But once I got here, I didn't know what to do." She reached down and opened her suitcase. "I've decided to go back. They will need me on Ylepithon."

Suddenly, she flipped open her ID case and held it upside down over the water. I just stood there, my mouth open, but Paul lunged to grab some of the hundreds of tiny golden discs as they fluttered out and caught the breeze. Sparkling in the sun like golden butterflies, they danced down into the creek.

Paul was aghast. "Galena, that was all of the knowledge on Earth! Why did you throw it away?"

A sigh escaped from Galena's translator box. "I've learned all I need to know." She snapped the suitcase shut.

Paul was still staring at the water, watching the disks twinkle in the sunlight as they bobbed along in the current. "Some school of fish will be well educated, that's for sure," he muttered.

"What would you have done with them anyway?" I asked, bending over so Galena could scramble up onto my back for a piggyback home.

Paul started to laugh. "You know what? I think I'd have swallowed them—just to see if I could digest some of the knowledge that way."

"Very funny!" I commented, trudging back up the trail. "The only knowledge you'd likely have acquired is what it feels like to have a gigantic bellyache!"

CHAPTER 19

I lovingly ran my hands over *Winnie the Pooh*, *Charlotte's Web*, and *Anne of Green Gables* for the last time before packing them into Galena's little suitcase. I hated to part with them, but Galena needed them more than I did. I knew she would want to teach the people on Ylepithon the magic of reading.

"I wish there was more room for gifts, Galena. There's so much I'd like to put in here. Kind of like a time capsule—from Earth, you know?"

"You have given me the most important gift already, Lisa."

Tucking her clean little space suits in around the books, I looked up. "I have? What?" But Galena, in her mysterious way, wouldn't answer.

Paul had phoned home and asked Auntie Teresa if he could spend the day at our place. We wanted Galena with us for all of her last day on Earth. Mom laughed that Galena was like a purple growth on my back. Wherever I went and whatever I did, she was there.

I did a lot of thinking throughout the day. At first, I felt guilty for having left Galena alone so much. Then I realized how much she'd learned about life on our planet.

In early evening, when Galena went with us to do chores and check on Copper and Butterscotch, I watched her communicate with the alpacas. I thought how she'd grown fond of Roper and how much she liked books. It dawned on me that she'd learned more than Gagar could ever have anticipated.

After Paul said good-bye, I sat down and wrote the following note to put in Galena's suitcase:

Note to Gagar
    I think Galena has learned what love is. I know she loves to read. She loves the alpacas. She loves Roper.
    And I think she loves me.
    Please let her teach you and other Ylepithons what love is.
    Signed, Love
                    Lisa

P.S. I'm sorry about the hair. Galena will explain.

I stayed up late pretending to do homework.

After I was sure that the adults were asleep, I took Galena down to say good-bye to the alpacas and to check on Butterscotch and Copper once more. I'd really hoped my cria would be born before Galena left, but it just wasn't meant to be.

We'd planned on sleeping for a few hours before the alarm went off at 2:00 a.m., but in the end, Galena and Roper and I were all too excited to sleep. I read some stories to Galena, and she insisted on reading a picture book about a dog to Roper, who seemingly found it very interesting. He lay with his head on his crossed paws, with a glazed look in his eyes, as Galena's translator box chimed out the story.

At 2:30 a.m. Galena gazed out the window at the stars. I think she was beginning to look forward to going home. With a whine, Roper scratched at the door.

"Shhh. I know Roper. It's time to go. We don't want to wake anyone." I picked up Galena's suitcase and took her by the hand. Her other arm clutched Tedu tightly. Noiselessly, we tiptoed downstairs.

Tiffy slept on her customary chair by the kitchen table. At the sight of Roper, whom she associated with Galena, she slunk off the chair, and ran to hide behind the couch. At least Roper wouldn't have to worry about her chasing him anymore.

The night was warm and crystal clear. Above us, the Big Dipper and the Milky Way glittered and twinkled. Somewhere nearby, insects serenaded. We stood close together in silence at the edge of the lawn.

Suddenly a sort of energy charged the air. Roper whined uneasily. The insects' chirping stopped. For a moment, dead silence rang in my ears. Then the trees began to whisper. Galena squeezed my hand.

"It's time," she said.

She threw her arms around Roper, burying her face in his fur. The coloured lights on her belt raced in circles.

As the air filled with a high pitched hum, a blinding light descended. I knelt down beside Roper, who cowered by my feet.

Galena entwined her arms about my neck as we hugged each other wordlessly.

I heard a door zip open and a ramp thunk to the ground. A shadowy figure inside the spaceship beckoned to Galena. She picked up her little suitcase and ran towards the ship, waving to me one last time.

"I love you, Lisa . . ." The words floated softly back to me, swirling through the high-pitched hum. Or was it the wind in the trees playing tricks on me?

Seconds later, as I clutched Roper, the space ship took off in a blaze of blinding, whirling light.

We sat silent for a moment in the starlit yard. Then, feeling empty, I tiptoed back upstairs to bed.

CHAPTER 20

L isa, wake up!" I opened one eye to squint at the clock. Roper jumped off the bed. It was 7:00 a.m. and it was Sunday. It felt like I'd just fallen asleep after seeing Galena off. I didn't want to wake up!

There was a knock on the door, and Dr. Ferguson's—Ted's voice again. "Lisa, wake up. You have to see what's in the pasture!"

Instantly, I was wide awake. My cria had been born!

"Coming!" I yelled, already half way into the heap of rumpled clothes I'd worn last night.

Still damp to the touch, the cria was only minutes old. It was struggling to get up for its first steps while Dr. Ferguson—Ted—checked it over. Butterscotch hovered nearby, sniffing at the baby, and humming.

"Oh, Tad . . . " It just slipped out. I'd meant to call him "Ted", and it got all mixed up with "Dad'" in my mind just before I said it. He probably was going to be a better dad than I'd had before, and

I didn't really feel comfortable calling him "Ted". That was Mom's name for him.

"Do you mind if I call you Tad?" I asked.

He seemed to read my mind. He smiled. "No, that would be fine."

"It's a girl. Look, Tad!" I pointed to the two little rows of nipples on her belly. This was almost too good to be true.

"Yes, and she's a healthy girl, too. Just look at her coat!" He parted her curly, white fluff with his hands. Underneath, it was a light apricot like Butterscotch. "I'll bet this little lady will be a real show stopper!"

I buried my face in her sweet smelling fibre, before kissing her little wet nose. She gazed at me with big, dark, unafraid eyes, then struggled again to get up.

"Just a minute, little one. You can find Mom and nurse in a few minutes. First we want to dip your navel with iodine, and then teach you not to be afraid of us," Tad said. He showed me how to rub her briskly from head to toe, flexing each leg until it relaxed, and even rubbing between her two toes and over the soft little pads of her feet.

"No more kissing, Lisa. This is business. We want her to remember our touch and not be afraid, but we don't want her to become confused and think she's a person rather than an alpaca."

We worked on her together for a few minutes.

"You know, Lisa, you've proven yourself very responsible recently. Your mother's going to be very busy when the baby arrives. I'm wondering if you'd like to work with me in the clinic as my assistant."

"Would I! What about the other chores I do?" I couldn't let my school work slip now that I'd started doing well.

"I've been thinking about that. I imagine Paul would like the job."

We sat in the grass watching the cria stand on wobbly legs. She started to nuzzle Butterscotch, who clucked encouragingly.

"Is there any way you could hire two people?" I asked.

Tad looked at me, "I guess we could. We probably need more help around here than I realize. Why?"

"Well, Brad...from my class... His family needs some extra money and...well..." I remembered the care he'd taken in cutting out his pictures and the way he'd taken Roper for walks. "I'm sure he'd do a good job," I added.

"I'll take your word for it. You can phone them both later to see when they can come over to talk about it."

We watched the cria until we were sure by the

white around her mouth that she was nursing.

"Where's Mom?" I asked.

Tad laughed. "I told her to sleep in this morning. When I saw that cria, my only thought was to wake you. Let's go tell her, or she'll never forgive us."

Following Tad up the path to the house, I put my hand in my pocket. My hand felt something silky and soft.

Pulling it out, I stared at it. One of Galena's locks of hair! She must have left it for me so I wouldn't forget her, as if that were possible. I'd place it in a special spot in my dresser drawer beside the golden grasshopper.

In fairytales, things often happen in threes. Maybe I should keep another spot open, just in case. Who knows?

I caught up to Tad as he opened the gate.

"You know what I'm going to call my cria?" I asked.

"Nope. With your creative mind though, I can hardly wait to hear."

I grinned. "Well, you know how registered animals always have fancy names? Her registration paper is going to say Galena's Goldilocks. But I'll just call her Goldilocks."

"Speaking of Galena, where is she this morning?" Tad asked.

"Oh, she had important things to do elsewhere. She's gone." I said. Looking up at the clouds in the sky, I could almost see her holding someone on her lap, her arms tucked tightly around their tummy, as she read a book.

Tad smiled. "Galena's Goldilocks, eh? I like that." He reached down to scratch Roper's head. "Come on, boy, let's go wake Mom and have some breakfast."

Author's Note

Thank you to the 1996 Grade Five
students at Webber Rd. Elementary for
their help in "baby-sitting" Galena when
she first arrived on Earth.

Rosemary Nelson
with a five-minute-old cria

Rosemary Nelson lives on a beautiful farm in the Okanagan Valley in British Columbia, where she and her husband raise alpacas. She is also a teacher-librarian in a local school. After raising her own family, she turned her hand and mind to an early love, creative writing. As well as publishing the two-part series for children of *The Golden Grasshopper* and *Galena's Gift*, Rosemary has also published with Napoleon the immensely popular *Dragon in the Clouds* (1994). She is currently working on her first young adult novel.